THE PERFECT LIE

LURING (Book #3)
TAKING (Book #4)
STALKING (Book #5)

RILEY PAIGE MYSTERY SERIES

ONCE GONE (Book #1)
ONCE TAKEN (Book #2)
ONCE CRAVED (Book #3)
ONCE LURED (Book #4)
ONCE HUNTED (Book #5)
ONCE PINED (Book #6)
ONCE FORSAKEN (Book #7)
ONCE COLD (Book #8)
ONCE STALKED (Book #9)
ONCE LOST (Book #10)
ONCE BURIED (Book #11)
ONCE BOUND (Book #12)
ONCE TRAPPED (Book #13)
ONCE DORMANT (Book #14)
ONCE SHUNNED (Book #15)
ONCE MISSED (Book #16)
ONCE CHOSEN (Book #17)

MACKENZIE WHITE MYSTERY SERIES

BEFORE HE KILLS (Book #1)
BEFORE HE SEES (Book #2)
BEFORE HE COVETS (Book #3)
BEFORE HE TAKES (Book #4)
BEFORE HE NEEDS (Book #5)
BEFORE HE FEELS (Book #6)
BEFORE HE SINS (Book #7)
BEFORE HE HUNTS (Book #8)
BEFORE HE PREYS (Book #9)
BEFORE HE LONGS (Book #10)
BEFORE HE LAPSES (Book #11)

BEFORE HE ENVIES (Book #12)
BEFORE HE STALKS (Book #13)
BEFORE HE HARMS (Book #14)

AVERY BLACK MYSTERY SERIES
CAUSE TO KILL (Book #1)
CAUSE TO RUN (Book #2)
CAUSE TO HIDE (Book #3)
CAUSE TO FEAR (Book #4)
CAUSE TO SAVE (Book #5)
CAUSE TO DREAD (Book #6)

KERI LOCKE MYSTERY SERIES
A TRACE OF DEATH (Book #1)
A TRACE OF MUDER (Book #2)
A TRACE OF VICE (Book #3)
A TRACE OF CRIME (Book #4)
A TRACE OF HOPE (Book #5)

THE PERFECT LIE

(A Jessie Hunt Psychological Suspense Thriller—Book Five)

BLAKE PIERCE

BLAKE PIERCE

Blake Pierce is author of the bestselling RILEY PAGE mystery series, which includes sixteen books (and counting). Blake Pierce is also the author of the MACKENZIE WHITE mystery series, comprising thirteen books (and counting); of the AVERY BLACK mystery series, comprising six books; of the KERI LOCKE mystery series, comprising five books; of the MAKING OF RILEY PAIGE mystery series, comprising five books (and counting); of the KATE WISE mystery series, comprising six books (and counting); of the CHLOE FINE psychological suspense mystery, comprising five books (and counting); and of the JESSE HUNT psychological suspense thriller series, comprising five books (and counting).

ONCE GONE (a Riley Paige Mystery—Book #I), BEFORE HE KILLS (A Mackenzie White Mystery—Book I), CAUSE TO KILL (An Avery Black Mystery—Book I), A TRACE OF DEATH (A Keri Locke Mystery—Book I), and WATCHING (The Making of Riley Paige—Book I) are each available as a free download on Amazon!

An avid reader and lifelong fan of the mystery and thriller genres, Blake loves to hear from you, so please feel free to visit www.blakepierceauthor.com to learn more and stay in touch.

TABLE OF CONTENTS

CHAPTER ONE

Jessie almost had him.

The suspect was about ten yards ahead of her. They were both running on the sand, which felt surprisingly cold under her bare feet. The beach was virtually empty and she wondered when her backup would arrive. The suspect was bigger than her and if he turned around, she might have to shoot him to maintain her advantage. She wanted to avoid that if at all possible.

Suddenly, with the man almost in grasping distance, he seemed to collapse. But then she realized that he was actually sinking. A moment later he dropped through the sand right before her eyes.

Jessie barely had time to process that he'd fallen through a sinkhole on the beach before she felt herself being sucked down too. She tried to grab onto anything she could to prevent herself from falling into the hole. But there was nothing but loose sand. Still, she clung to it even as she disappeared under the dune.

When she regained consciousness, she realized she was in what seemed like a sea cave. She had no recollection of how she got there. She saw the suspect she'd been chasing lying on his stomach in the dirt across from her. He wasn't moving, likely knocked out.

Glancing around, she tried to get a better sense of her surroundings. It was only then that she realized she was standing up with her arms above her head. Her wrists were tied with a rope that was attached to the top of the cave wall. The rope was so tight that the tips of her toes barely touched the ground below.

As her head cleared, a horrifying realization hit her: she'd been in this position before. This was the exact scenario she'd faced two months ago when her own father, the brutal serial killer Xander Thurman, had captured and tortured her before she'd managed to kill him.

Was this some copycat killer? How was that even possible? The details of the incident had been kept secret. Then she heard a noise and saw a shadow in the mouth of the cave. As he stepped into view she tried to identify him. But he was backlit by the sun and his features were obscured. All she could see was the silhouette of a tall, thin man and the gleam of the long knife in his hand.

He stepped forward and kicked the body of the unconscious man in the sand that she'd been chasing earlier. He rolled over and she saw that he wasn't unconscious. He was dead. His throat had been slit roughly and blood covered his chest.

Jessie looked back up, still unable to see the face of her captor. In the background, she heard a quiet groaning. She looked in the corner of the cave and noticed something she'd missed earlier. A young woman, in her teens, was tied to a chair with her mouth gagged. She was the one groaning. Her terrified eyes were wide.

This too seemed impossible. It was just what had happened before. Another girl had been tied up just like this in that last encounter. That had also been kept secret. And yet the man approaching her now seemed to know every detail. He was only a few feet from her when she finally saw his face and gasped.

It was her father.

That was unfathomable. She had killed him herself in a brutal fight. She remembered crushing his skull with her legs. Had that been an imposter? Had he somehow survived? It seemed irrelevant as he lifted the knife and prepared to plunge it into her.

She tried to get better footing so she could leap up and kick him backward but her feet wouldn't reach the ground no matter how hard she stretched. Her father looked at her with an expression of amused pity.

"Did you think I would make the same mistake twice, Junebug?" he asked.

Then, without another word, he swung the knife down, aiming it directly at her heart. She closed her eyes tight, preparing for the death blow.

She gasped as she felt a sharp twinge, not in her chest but in her back.

Jessie opened her tightly clenched eyes to discover that she was not in a sea cave at all but in her own sweat-drenched bed in her downtown Los Angeles apartment. Somehow, she was sitting upright.

She glanced over at the clock and saw that it was 2:51 a.m. The pain in her back was not from a recent stab wound but rather the intensity of her final physical therapy session earlier today. But the lingering soreness originally came from her father's real attack eight weeks ago.

He had sliced through her flesh from just below her right shoulder blade down to near her kidney, mowing through muscle and sinew. The subsequent surgery required thirty-seven stitches.

Gingerly, she got out of bed and made her way to the bathroom. Once there she looked in the mirror and took stock of her wounds. Her eyes passed right over the scar on the left side of her abdomen, a permanent gift of her ex-husband and a fireplace poker. She also barely noticed the childhood scar that ran along much of her collarbone, a remnant of her father's knife.

Instead, she focused on the multiple injuries she'd suffered in the actual death match with her father. He'd sliced into her multiple times, especially around the legs, leaving scars that would never go away and would make wearing a bathing suit without getting shocked stares a challenging proposition.

The worst blow was to her right thigh, where he'd stabbed her in a final, unsuccessful attempt to break free from the knees that were crushing his temples. She was no longer limping but still felt mild discomfort every time she put pressure on the leg, which meant every time she took a step. The physical therapist said there was some nerve damage and that while the pain would decrease over the next few months, it might never completely subside.

Despite that, she had been cleared to return to work as a forensic profiler for the LAPD. Her first day back was supposed to be tomorrow, which might help explain the extra-vivid nightmare. She'd had lots of others but this was an award-winner.

She tied her shoulder-length brown hair back in a ponytail and, with her penetrating green eyes, studied her face. So far, it was free of scars and, so she'd been told, was still quite striking. At a lean, athletic five foot ten, she'd often been mistaken for a sports model, though she doubted she'd be doing lingerie work anytime soon. Still, for someone about to turn thirty who'd been through as much as she had, she thought she was holding up pretty well.

She walked to the kitchen, poured herself a glass of water, and sat down at the breakfast table, resigned to the likelihood that she wouldn't be getting much more sleep tonight. She was used to sleepless nights back when she had two serial killers searching for her. But now one of them was dead and the other had apparently decided to leave her be. So theoretically she should be able to really catch up. But it didn't seem to work that way.

Part of it was that she couldn't be one hundred percent certain that the other serial killer who'd taken an interest in her, Bolton Crutchfield, was really gone for good. All indications were that he was. No one had seen or heard from him since her own final sighting of him eight weeks ago. Not a single lead had emerged.

More importantly, she knew he was fond of her in a non-murdery kind of way. Her multiple interviews with him in his cell before he'd escaped had established a connection. He'd actually warned her about the threat from her own father on two occasions, putting himself in his one-time mentor's crosshairs. He seemed to have moved on from her. So why couldn't she? Why wouldn't she allow herself to get a good night's sleep?

Part of it was probably that she couldn't *ever* let anything go. Part of it was that she was still in some physical discomfort. Part of it was almost certainly that she would be starting work again in about five hours and likely working again with Detective Ryan Hernandez, for whom her feelings were, to put it mildly, complicated.

Sighing in resignation, Jessie officially made the transition from water to coffee. As she waited for it to brew, she wandered around the apartment, her third in the last two months, checking to make sure all the doors and windows were locked.

This was supposed to be her new, semi-permanent address and she was pretty happy with it. After bouncing around from one sterile U.S. Marshal Service–approved location to another, she'd finally been allowed to have a say in what was intended to be her long-term living quarters. The Service had helped find the place and ensured its security.

The apartment was in a twenty-story building only blocks from her last real apartment in the fashion district section of downtown L.A. The building had its own full security team, not just a single guard in the lobby. There were always three guards on duty, one of whom patrolled the parking garage while another made regular rounds on the various floors.

The parking garage was secured by a gate manned 24/7 by an on-duty attendant. The rotating doorman was all retired cops. There was a metal detector built into the dedicated non-resident entryway to the building. All elevators and units had dual key fob and fingerprint access requirements. Every floor of the complex, including the on-site laundry facilities, gym, and pool, had multiple security cameras. Every unit had alert buttons and direct intercom access to the security desk. And that was just the stuff the building provided.

It didn't account for her service weapon or for the additional security measures the Marshals had helped her set up inside the unit. They included shatterproof, bulletproof glass for the windows and sliding patio door, a double-thick front door that required a law-enforcement-level battering ram to knock off its hinges, and interior motion-activated and heat-sensing cameras that could be turned on or off using her phone.

Finally, there was one last precaution, Jessie's favorite. She actually lived on the thirteenth floor, even though, like in many buildings, it supposedly didn't exist. There was no button for it on the elevator. The service elevator could get to the floor but required a security guard to accompany anyone using it. To access the floor under normal circumstances, one had to get off on level twelve or fourteen and open a nondescript door off the main hallway marked "service panel entry."

That door did actually lead to a small room with the service panel. But in the back of the room was an additional door marked "storage," which required a special key fob. That door led to a stairwell that accessed the thirteenth floor, which was comprised of eight apartments, just like the other floors.

But each of these units was occupied by someone who clearly placed a premium on privacy, security, or both. In the week that Jessie had been here, she'd encountered one well-known television actress, a high-profile whistleblower attorney, and a controversial radio talk show host in the halls.

Jessie, who had done well in her divorce, wasn't concerned about the cost. And because of some law enforcement discounts the LAPD and Marshal Service had secured on her behalf, it wasn't as expensive as she'd expected. Regardless, it was worth it to have the peace of mind. Of course, she'd thought her last place had been secure too.

Her coffee machine beeped and she went over to pour a cup. As she prepped it, adding cream and sugar, she wondered if any special measures had been taken to protect Hannah Dorsey. Hannah was the real seventeen-year-old girl who'd been tied up and gagged by Xander Thurman, forced to watch as he murdered her parents and almost killed Jessie.

Jessie's thoughts turned to Hannah often, in part because she wondered how the girl was doing in her foster home after suffering such trauma. Jessie had gone through something similar when she was a girl, though she'd been much younger, only six. Xander had tied her up in an isolated cabin and forced her to watch as he tortured and killed her mom, his own wife.

The experience had left her permanently scarred and she was sure the same would be true for Hannah. Of course, what this girl didn't know, what she was blessed to be unaware of, was that Xander was her father too, which meant that she was Jessie's half-sister.

According to authorities, Hannah knew that she was adopted but had no knowledge of her real parents' identity. And since Jessie had been forbidden to meet with her after their shared ordeal, the girl had no idea that they were related. Despite her pleas to talk to the girl and her promise not to reveal their connection, everyone in authority agreed that they should not meet again until the doctors felt Hannah could handle it.

Intellectually, Jessie understood the decision and even agreed with it. But somewhere deeper, she felt the strong urge to talk to the girl. They had so much in common. Their father was a monster. Their mothers were mysteries. Hannah had never met hers and Jessie's was only a distant memory. And just as Xander had killed Hannah's adoptive parents, he'd done the same to Jessie's.

Despite all that, they were not alone. Each had a family connection that could offer solace and some hope for recovery. Each had a sister, something that Jessie had never even imagined possible. She yearned to reach out and create some bond with the only other surviving member of her bloodline.

And yet, even as she wished for a reunion, she couldn't help but wonder.

Would knowing me do this girl more harm than good?

CHAPTER TWO

The man skulked down the apartment complex's outdoor hallway, looking over his shoulder every few seconds. It was early in the morning and a guy like him, thick as a tank, African-American and wearing a hoodie, tended to draw attention.

He was on the eighth floor, just outside the apartment of the woman he knew lived here. He also knew what her car looked like and had seen it in the parking garage below, so he assumed she might be in. As a precaution, the man knocked softly on the front door.

It wasn't even seven a.m. yet and he didn't want any early riser neighbors to poke their curious heads out. It was cold outside this morning and the man didn't want to take off the hoodie. But fearing it would draw too much attention, he pulled it off his head, exposing his skin to the biting wind.

When he got no response to his knock, he made a perfunctory attempt to open the door he was sure would be locked. It was. He moved over to the adjacent window. He could see that it was slightly open. He debated whether he should really go ahead with this. After a moment's hedging he made up his mind, yanked the window up, and climbed in. He knew anyone who saw him would likely be calling the cops but decided it was worth the risk.

Once inside, he tried to make his way quietly to the bedroom. All the lights were off and there was a strange smell he couldn't identify. As he stepped further back into the apartment, he got a cold chill that had nothing to do with the weather. He reached the door of the bedroom, gently turned the knob, and peeked in.

There on the bed was the woman he'd been expecting to see. She appeared to be sleeping but something was weird. Even in the dim morning light, her skin looked strangely pale. Also, she didn't seem to be moving at all. No rising and

7

falling of the chest. No movement at all. He stepped into the room and walked over to the bed. The smell was overwhelming now, a rotting stench that made his eyes water and his stomach turn.

He wanted to reach out and touch her but couldn't bring himself to. He wanted to say something but couldn't find the words. Finally he turned away and stepped out of the room.

He pulled out his phone and dialed the only number he could think of. It rang several times before giving him a recorded voice. He pushed several buttons and waited for a response as he retreated to the living room of the apartment. Finally, a voice came on the line.

"911. What is your emergency?"

"Yes, my name is Vin Stacey. I think my friend is dead. Her name is Taylor Jansen. I came to her apartment because I couldn't reach her for several days. She's lying in her bed. But she isn't moving and she . . . doesn't look right. Also there's a smell."

That was the moment when the reality of the situation hit him—that vivacious, enthusiastic Taylor was lying dead less than thirty feet from him. He bent over and threw up.

⚜   ⚜   ⚜

Jessie sat in the back seat for what she hoped was the final time. The U.S. Marshal vehicle pulled into the LAPD Central Station parking structure and parked in a visitor spot. Standing there waiting was her boss, Captain Roy Decker.

He didn't look much different than the last time she saw him. Almost sixty, though he appeared much older, Decker was tall and skinny with a mostly bald head, deep creases in his face, a sharp nose, and small, penetrating eyes. He was talking to a uniformed officer but was clearly there to meet her.

"Wow," she said sarcastically to the Marshals in the front seat. "I feel like a woman in the eighteenth century being formally handed off from her father to her husband."

The Marshal in the passenger seat scowled back at her. His name was Patrick Murphy, though everyone called him Murph. Short and trim, with tightly cropped light brown hair, he projected a no-nonsense sensibility, though that turned out to be a bit of ruse.

"That scenario would require a husband who wanted to take you in, which I find highly unlikely," said the man who had coordinated much of her security while she on the run from multiple serial killers.

Only the slightest hint of a grin at the edges of his mouth hinted that he was joking.

"You are, as always, a prince among men, Murph," she said, faux-politely. "I don't know how I'm going to muddle through without your charming personage at my side."

"Me either," he muttered.

"Nor without your conversational charisma, Marshal Toomey," she said to the driver, a massive man with a shaved head and a blank expression.

Toomey, who rarely spoke, nodded silently.

Captain Decker, who had finished talking to the officer, looked at the three of them impatiently, waiting for them to get out of the car.

"I guess this is it," Jessie said, opening the door and getting out with more energy than she felt. "How's it going, Captain?"

"More complicated today than yesterday," he said, "now that I've got you back on my hands."

"But I swear, Captain, Murph here has collected a hefty dowry to go along with me. I promise not to be a burden and to always earn my wifely keep."

"What?" he asked, perplexed.

"Oh, Pa," she said, turning back to Murph. "Do I have to leave the farm? I'll miss you and Mother ever so much."

"What the hell is going on?" Decker demanded.

Murph forced his face into a mask of seriousness and turned to the confused cop who had walked over to the passenger window.

"Captain Decker," he said formally, handing over clipboard with a sheet of paper on it. "The protection duty of the U.S. Marshal Service is no longer required. I hereby officially relinquish custody of Jessie Hunt to the Los Angeles Police Department."

"Custody?" Jessie repeated testily. Murph, ignoring her, continued.

"Any additional security measures are now the obligation of your department. Signing this document acknowledges such."

Decker took the clipboard and signed the paper without reading it. Then he handed it back and looked at Jessie.

"Good news, Hunt," he said gruffly, without any of the enthusiasm that usually accompanied good news. "The detectives trying to track down Bolton Crutchfield found video footage of someone matching his description crossing the Mexican border yesterday. You may finally be free of the guy."

"Facial recognition confirmed it?" she asked skeptically, losing the fake voice for the first time.

"No," he admitted. "He kept his head down the entire time he walked across the bridge. But he matches the physical description almost perfectly and the very fact that he took care never to be cleanly captured in video suggests he knew what he was doing."

"That *is* good news," she said, deciding not to comment beyond that.

She agreed that she was likely no longer in Crutchfield's crosshairs, but not because of some sketchy surveillance video that seemed far too convenient. Of course, she didn't feel like she could tell Decker the real reason was her hunch that the killer had a soft spot for her.

"You ready to get back to work?" he asked, satisfied that he had addressed any lingering concerns she might have.

"In just a minute, Captain," she said. "I just need a quick word with the marshals."

"Make it fast," Decker said as he walked several steps away. "You've got a busy day of sitting behind a desk ahead of you."

"Yes sir," she said before leaning down to the driver's window.

"I think I'll miss you most of all, Scarecrow," she said to Toomey, who'd been her primary assigned marshal for the last two months. He nodded back. Apparently no words were necessary. Then she walked around to the passenger side and looked at Murphy guiltily.

"All joking aside, I just wanted to say how much I appreciate everything you've done for me. You put yourselves on the line to keep me safe and I'll never forget it."

He was still on crutches, though the casts on his legs had been removed last week, replaced by soft boots. That was around the same time he was permitted to remove the sling around his arm.

All those injuries were a result of being hit by the car Xander Thurman was driving when he ambushed him and Jessie in an alley. He'd broken both legs and his clavicle. So officially, he was on leave from the service for another four months. He'd only come this morning to see her off.

"Don't start getting emotional on me now," he protested. "We've got this 'hard-bitten, reluctant allies' thing down cold. You're going to mess it up."

"How's Emerson's family doing?" she asked quietly.

Troy Emerson was the marshal her father had shot in the head that terrible night. Jessie hadn't even known his first name until after he died, nor that he was recently married with a four-month-old son. She hadn't been able to go to the funeral because of her injuries but had subsequently reached out to Emerson's widow. She hadn't heard back.

"Kelly's getting there," Murph assured her. "She got your message. I know she wants to get back to you but she just needs more time."

"I understand. To be honest, I'd understand if she never wanted to speak to me."

"Hey, don't take all this on yourself," he replied, almost angrily. "It's not your fault your dad was a psycho. And Troy knew the risks when he got into this job. We all did. You can feel sympathy. But don't feel guilty."

Jessie nodded, unable to think of a suitable response.

"I'd give you a hug," Murph said. "But it would make me wince, and not for emotional reasons. So let's just pretend we did, okay?"

"Whatever you say, Marshal Murphy," she said.

"Don't start getting formal on me now," he insisted as he delicately eased himself back into the passenger seat of the car. "You can still call me Murph. It's not like I'm going to stop calling you by your nickname."

"What's that?" she asked.

"The pain in my ass."

She couldn't help but laugh at that.

"Goodbye, Murph," she said. "Give Toomey a kiss for me."

"I'd do that even without being asked," he shouted as Toomey hit the accelerator and the tires squealed on the garage floor.

Jessie turned around to find Decker staring at her impatiently.

"You done?" he asked sharply. "Or should I take in a showing of *The Notebook* while you all work out your emotions some more?"

"It's good to be back, Captain," she sighed.

He started walking inside and waved for her to follow him. She ignored the twinge in her leg and back and jogged after him. She was only just catching up when he launched into his plan for her.

"So don't expect any fieldwork for a while," he said gruffly. "I wasn't kidding about keeping you on a desk. You're rusty and I can see you desperately trying not to limp on that right leg as you walk. Until I think you're solid again, you should get used the bullpen's fluorescent lights."

"Don't you think I'd get back in the swing of things quicker if I just dived in?" Jessie asked, trying not to sound pleading. She had to take two steps to every one of his to keep up as he barreled down the hall.

"Funny, that's almost exactly what your buddy Hernandez said when he came back last week. I put him on desk duty too. And guess what? He's still there."

"I didn't know Hernandez was back," she said.

"I thought you two were bosom buddies," he said as they rounded the corner.

Jessie glanced over at him sideways, trying to determine if her boss was suggesting anything. But he seemed to be sincere.

"We're friends," she acknowledged. "But I think with the injuries he suffered and his divorce, he wanted a little time to himself."

"Really?" Decker said. "You could have fooled me."

She didn't know what to make of that comment but didn't have time to ask before they arrived at the station bullpen, a large room filled with a mishmash of desks pushed together, all populated by various detectives representing different LAPD divisions. At the far end of the bullpen, with the other Homicide Special Section detectives, was Ryan Hernandez.

For a man who'd been stabbed twice only two months earlier by her father (it seemed that every injured person she knew these days got their wounds at the hands of her father), Hernandez looked pretty good.

His left forearm wasn't even bandaged anymore. The other wound had been to the left side of his abdomen. But considering that he was standing upright and laughing, she figured it couldn't be bothering him that much.

As Decker led her over, she found herself perplexed by how annoyed she was at Hernandez joking around. She should be happy that he wasn't depressed in the aftermath of having his marriage fall apart *and* nearly being killed. But if he was doing so well, why hadn't he reached out more than two perfunctory times in the last couple of months?

She'd made much more of an effort to check in and rarely heard back. She'd assumed it was because he was struggling and had given him space to regroup. But based on how he looked now, everything seemed to be peachy.

"Nice to see the Homicide Special Section is in such good spirits on this fine morning," Decker bellowed, startling the five men and one woman who comprised the unit. Detective Alan Trembley, looking as scattershot as usual, even dropped his bagel.

Homicide Special Section was a division assigned to high-profile cases, often ones with intense media scrutiny. That meant lots of homicides with multiple victims and serial killers. It was prestigious assignment and Hernandez was considered the cream of the crop.

"Look who's back," Detective Callum Reid said enthusiastically. "I didn't know you were returning today. Now we've finally got some class back in the joint."

"You know," Jessie said, deciding to embrace the vibe of the group, "you could be classy too, Reid, if you didn't let one rip every ten seconds. It's not a high bar."

Everyone busted out laughing.

"It's funny because it's true," Trembley said happily, his unkempt blond curls bouncing as he laughed. He pushed up his glasses, which perpetually slid down his nose.

"How you feeling, Jessie?" Hernandez said when the noise had died down.

"I'm getting by," she answered, trying not to sound cold. "You look like you're on the mend."

"Getting there," he said. "I've still got a few aches and pains. But as I keep telling the Captain here, if he'd let me in the game I could make a real difference. I'm tired of riding the bench, Coach."

"That never gets old, Hernandez," Decker said grumpily, clearly tired of the team analogy. "Hunt, I'll give you a few minutes to get resettled. Then we'll go over your case load. I have a bunch of unsolved homicide files that could use a fresh eye. Maybe a profiler's perspective will shake things up. I expect the rest of you to give me case updates in my office in five minutes. It looks like you have the spare time."

He headed for his office grumbling to himself. The rest of the team assembled their files as Hernandez plopped down across from Jessie.

"You don't have anything to report?" she asked.

"I don't have any cases of my own yet. I've been backing these guys up on everything. Maybe now that you're back, we can tag team Decker and get him to send us out on something. The two of us together make up one almost totally healthy person."

"I'm glad that you're in such good spirits," Jessie said, desperately trying to stop herself from saying more but failing to do so. "I wish you'd have let me know you were all good earlier. I steered clear because I thought you were working stuff out."

Hernandez's smile faded as he took in what she said. He seemed to be weighing how to respond. As she waited for his reply and despite her annoyance, Jessie couldn't help but admit the guy had maintained himself pretty well while recovering from a grievous injury and a divorce.

He looked put together. Not a strand of his short black hair was out of place. His brown eyes were clear and focused. And somehow, despite his injuries, he'd managed to keep in shape. He might have lost five pounds off his usual six-foot, two-hundred-pound frame, probably related to difficulty eating right after getting his stomach sliced open. But at thirty-one, he still had the toned look of a man who worked out often.

"Yeah, about that," he started to say, snapping her back into the moment. "I wanted to call, but the thing is, some stuff has been going on and I wasn't sure how to talk about it."

"What kind of stuff?" she asked nervously. She didn't like where this was headed.

Hernandez looked down, as if deciding how best to broach what was clearly a touchy subject. After a full five seconds he looked back up at her. Just as he was opening his mouth, Decker burst out of his office.

"We've got a gang-involved shooting in Westlake North," he shouted. "The scene is still active. We already have four fatalities and an unknown number of injuries. I need SWAT, HSS, and gang units en route now. This is all hands on deck, people!"

CHAPTER THREE

Immediately, everyone began tearing around the bullpen. Many headed for the tactical gear center, where they grabbed heavier artillery and bulletproof vests. Jessie and Hernandez looked at each other, unsure what to do. He started to get out of his seat when Decker shut him down.

"Don't even think about it, Hernandez. You're not getting anywhere near this thing."

Hernandez slumped back down in his chair. They watched the action around the station with jealous interest. After a few minutes, things quieted down and then remaining staff went back to work. Seemingly only moments ago, the bullpen had been bustling with activity, filled with well over fifty people. Now it was a ghost town. Including Jessie and Hernandez, there were fewer than ten left.

Suddenly Jessie heard a loud thud. She looked over to see that Captain Decker had dropped a half dozen thick files on her desk.

"These are the cases I want you to review," he said. "I had hoped to go over them with you but obviously I'm going to be busy for the next few hours."

"Any updates on the shooting?" she asked him.

"The shooting has stopped. Everyone scattered once our cars arrived. We're up to six fatalities, all from rival gangs. Another dozen or so are injured. We've got about thirty officers and a dozen detectives canvassing the area. And that doesn't even include SWAT."

"What about me?" Hernandez asked. "How can I help, Captain?"

"You can follow up on your colleagues' cases until they get back. I'm sure they'll be very appreciative. I've got to get back to this gang thing now."

He hurried back to his office, leaving the two of them alone except for the mounds of paperwork.

"I think he's being mean on purpose," Hernandez muttered.

"Did you want to finish what you were saying before?" Jessie asked him, wondering if she was pushing too hard.

"Not now," he replied, losing the lightness in his voice. "Maybe later, when we're out of the office and everything isn't so...heightened."

Jessie nodded in agreement, though she was disappointed. Rather than pout or stay in that unpleasant head space, she turned her attention to the case files in front of her.

Maybe focusing on the minutiae of some murders will clear my head.

She chuckled silently at her own gallows humor as she opened the first file.

It worked. She became so immersed in the details of the cases that almost an hour passed without her noticing the time. It wasn't until Hernandez tapped her on the shoulder that she looked up and realized it was mid-morning.

"I think I might have found us a case," he said, holding up a piece of paper provocatively.

"I thought we weren't supposed to be hunting for new cases," she replied.

"We're not," he admitted. "But there's no one else here to take it and I think it's the sort of thing Decker might actually let us take on."

He held out the paper. Not as reluctantly as she probably should have, Jessie took it. It didn't take her long to realize why they might have a shot at convincing Decker to let them take it.

The case seemed pretty straightforward. A thirty-year-old woman was found dead in her Hollywood apartment. The young man who first reported finding her was initially held on suspicion when a neighbor reported seeing him enter the apartment through a window. But he asserted he was a co-worker who was checking on her after not hearing from her for two days. There were no obvious signs of violence and the initial impression on the scene was that this was likely a suicide.

"It seems like they have things pretty well in hand. I'm not sure what we can offer...."

"I hear a silent 'but' in there," Hernandez noted, smiling.

Jessie didn't want to give him the satisfaction but found herself grinning slightly too.

"But...there is a reference to older bruising on her wrists and neck, which might suggest previous abuse. That's probably worth checking out. And according to her co-worker, she worked as a personal trainer at a high-end fitness club, where she specialized in high-profile clients. It's possible some of them will make a stink if they think LAPD isn't putting enough resources into the case."

"Exactly," Hernandez said excitedly. "That's our 'in,' Jessie. If I know Decker, he's not going to risk alienating the hoi polloi if he can avoid it. Assigning a detective from HSS and a celebrated forensic profiler to the case short-circuits that criticism. Plus, it seems pretty ideal for easing us back into the field. There's no sign of violence. If it was murder, we're probably talking poisoning or something along those lines. It seems like a largely stabbing-free case."

"He was pretty adamant that we stick to desks for a while," Jessie reminded him.

"I think he'll go for it," Hernandez insisted. "Besides, he's so distracted with the gang shooting, he might say yes just to get rid of us. Let's at least try."

"I'll go with you," Jessie said. "But I'm not making the pitch. If he cuts anyone's head off, it's going to be yours."

"Coward," he teased.

Jessie had to admit that Ryan Hernandez was good.

He barely had to say more than the words "wealthy clients," "Hollywood," and "likely suicide" before Decker was ushering them out the door to pursue the case. Those buzzwords hit all their boss's weak spots: his fear of bad publicity, his ongoing goal not to alienate his supervisors, and his deep desire not to have Detective Hernandez pester him relentlessly.

His only rule was simple.

"If it starts to look like this *is* a murder and the perpetrator used any kind of force, call me for backup."

Now, as Hernandez drove them to Hollywood, he looked almost giddy with excitement. So did his foot.

"Careful on the gas there, Earnhardt," she warned. "I don't want to get in an accident on the way to the scene."

She said nothing about their discussion from earlier, deciding to let him bring it up when he was ready. It didn't take long. After the initial rush of being in a car on the way to crime scene faded, he glanced in her direction.

"So here's the deal," he started, his words tumbling out much faster than normal. "I should have reached out to you more often after everything went down. I mean, I did at first obviously. But you were badly hurt and not very chatty, which I completely understand."

"Do you?" Jessie asked skeptically.

"Of course," he said as he exited the 101 freeway at Vine Street. "You had to kill your own father. Even if he was a psycho, he was your dad. But I wasn't sure how to broach that with you. And there was the fact that your psycho dad stabbed me. That wasn't your fault but I was worried you would think I blamed you. So I was thinking all those things while having my stomach leak blood periodically and being heavily doped up on pain medication *and* trying keep food down. And right when I thought I was ready to discuss all that in an adult way, my wife formally served me with divorce papers. It was already going to happen. But there was something about getting those legal documents, especially while I was still in the hospital—it kind of wrecked me. I went down this black hole. I didn't want to eat. I didn't want to rehab. I didn't want to talk to anyone, which is exactly what I *should* have been doing."

"I can recommend someone if…"Jessie started to offer.

"Thank you but I'm all set actually," he interrupted. "Decker finally ordered me to see someone—said I was in danger of not coming back at all if I didn't get my shit together. So I did. And it helped. But by then, it had been about six weeks since the attack and it felt weird to just call you out of the blue. And to be honest, I wasn't 100% sure I was okay … psychologically, and I didn't want to lose it while talking to you seriously for the first time after we both almost died. So I pushed it off some more. And then there's the other thing."

"What other thing?"

"You know, our whole 'friendly co-workers but also friends who sometimes get awkward because maybe there's something there' thing? I'm not imagining that, right?"

Jessie took a long beat before responding. Answering this honestly would change things. But he was laying it all out there. It felt gutless not to do the same.

"No, you're not imagining that."

He laughed uncomfortably, which turned into a full-on, eye-watering cough.

"You okay?" she asked.

"Yeah, I'm just … I was nervous to mention that last part."

They sat in silence for a minute as he navigated the traffic on Sunset Boulevard, trying to find a spot to park.

"So that's the deal?" she finally said.

"That's the deal," he confirmed as he pulled into a spot.

"You know," she said gently. "You are nowhere near as cool as I first thought you were."

"It's all a front," he said, half-joking but clearly only half.

"I kind of like it. It makes you more . . . approachable."

"Thanks, I guess."

"Well, we should probably talk about this a little more," she replied.

"I think that would be the mature thing to do," he agreed. "You do mean after we check out the dead body upstairs, right?"

"Yes, Ryan. Dead body first. Awkward conversation later."

CHAPTER FOUR

It was like a light turned on in Jessie's head.

The second she shut the car door and looked at the building that currently housed a dead woman, her mind cleared. All thoughts of serial killer fathers, orphaned half-sisters, and semi-romantic possibilities faded into the background.

She and Ryan stood on the sidewalk near the corner of Sunset and Vine, taking in the area. This was the heart of Hollywood and Jessie had been here many times. But that was always to go to dinner, a concert, or to see a movie or live show. She'd never really focused on it as a place where regular people worked, lived, and apparently died.

For the first time she noticed that among the office towers, restaurants, and theaters many of the buildings were just like the mixed-use ones in her neighborhood, with retail businesses on the ground floor and apartments or condos on the ones above.

Just up the street, she saw a ten-story apartment complex with a Trader Joe's below it. Just across the street was a Solstice Fitness Center at the base of a building easily twenty stories tall. She wondered if residents got complimentary memberships but doubted it. That place was unbelievably pricey.

It looked like the victim's complex was slightly less upscale. It had several restaurants and a yoga studio on the first floor. But there was also a Walgreens and a Bed, Bath & Beyond. As they walked along the sidewalk to the main entrance, they had to sidestep a line of homeless people camped out along the wall of the building. Most weren't awake yet, though one older woman was sitting cross-legged, muttering to herself.

They passed her without comment and arrived at the entrance to the building. Compared to Jessie's building, the security here was a joke. There was a glass vestibule entrance that required an access card and another to summon the elevator. But when Jessie and Ryan were approaching the entrance, a resident held the door open for them and swiped the elevator sensor without asking them a thing. Jessie noticed fixed cameras in the vestibule and on the elevator but they looked cheap. Ryan pushed the button for the eighth floor and within seconds they were stepping out, never having been challenged.

"That was easy," Ryan said as they walked down the exterior hall in the direction of the police tape and several officers milling about.

"Way too easy," Jessie noted. "I realize I'm a crazy person when it comes to personal security. But this place is pretty pathetic, especially considering the neighborhood."

"It's a lot safer than it was twenty years ago," Ryan reminded her.

"True. But just because you don't have hookers and drug dealers in plain sight on every corner doesn't mean it's Disneyland now."

Ryan didn't respond as they had reached the victim's apartment. He flashed his detective's badge and she showed her LAPD profiler ID.

"Detectives from Hollywood Division have already come and gone," a perplexed officer said.

"We're just following up for Homicide Special Section," Ryan lied. "It's mostly a favor for our captain. We'd appreciate if you'd have someone walk us through the scene, even if they have to repeat stuff."

"No problem," he replied. "Officer Wayne is primary on the scene. I'll get him."

As he radioed to the other officer, Jessie took in her surroundings. The front door was open now, as was a window adjacent to it. She wondered if it had been that way before. It was hard to imagine a single woman in the heart of Hollywood would leave a window open when it was accessible by an exterior hallway. It was almost an invitation to trouble.

The victim's unit was at the far end of the floor from the elevators, which was shaped like a blocky letter "C." That meant her apartment was visible to people across the open expanse between the halls. She was curious as to whether anyone had canvassed those units yet.

Just then, an older uniformed officer stepped out of the apartment to greet them. He was heavyset and balding, with stray hairs that had adhered to his sweaty scalp. He looked to be in his early forties and had that "seen it all" vibe that could be a help or a hindrance depending on his attitude.

"Officer John Wayne," he said extending his hand to Ryan. "I've already heard every joke you want to say, so you can skip it. What can I do for you?"

"You're the spitting image," Ryan couldn't help but say.

Jessie punched him in the arm before returning her attention to the cop, who looked unfazed.

"Sorry, Officer Wayne," she said. "Thanks for taking the time. We know the Hollywood detectives have already worked the scene. But we were hoping you could show us around anyway. This case has hallmarks that match something we're working on and we want to rule it out as connected."

"Of course, come on in," he said, stepping back inside and handing them plastic shoe covers as they prepared to enter.

They put them on, along with gloves, and walked in.

"Some of her possessions have already been booked as evidence," Wayne said. "But we can give you an itemized list."

"Anything jump out at you?" Ryan asked.

"A few things," the officer replied. "No sign of forced entry. There was money in her purse. Her phone was on the bedside table."

"If you don't mind," Jessie asked, "before you give us the rest of the rundown, I'd like to take a moment to evaluate the site without any preconceptions."

Officer Wayne nodded. Jessie took a long deep breath, allowed her body to relax and began to profile the victim. The living room was sparsely decorated with furniture that looked to have been purchased from IKEA. There was limited artwork and no visible photos. The only personal touch was a framed NASM personal training certification on the wall.

She walked into the almost untouched kitchen. There were no dirty dishes in the sink nor clean ones on the drying rack. One clean, folded dish towel rested on the counter. Next to it were several pill containers, each marked with days of the week, each painstakingly laid out in order. Jessie didn't touch them but from what she could tell, the pills inside looked like supplements and multivitamins. She noticed that neither the pills for Monday nor Tuesday had been taken. This was Wednesday morning.

She looked around the rest of the kitchen. The paper towel roll was almost full. Opening the cabinets revealed dozens of cans of beans and ground turkey, lots of protein bars and multiple vats of whey protein powder.

The refrigerator was half empty but the contents included two gallon-sized jugs of milk, several containers of Greek yogurt and a massive plastic bag of spinach. The freezer was a mix of frozen blueberries, strawberries and acai and a Tupperware container of what looked like chicken noodle soup. Taped to the outside of it was a Post-it that read "from Mom, 11/2018." That was well over a year ago.

The three of them wandered down the hall toward the bedroom where the body was waiting. The smell of rotting flesh enveloped Jessie's nostrils. She allowed herself a moment to accept it, then made a pit stop in the bathroom, which wasn't as tidy as the rest of the house. It was clear the resident spent much more time in here.

"What was the victim's name?" she asked. It had been on the document Ryan had given her at the station but she had purposely avoided noting it until now.

"Taylor Jansen," Officer Wayne said. "She was . . ."

"Sorry, Officer," she interrupted. "I don't want to be rude but please hold off on any other details just a bit longer."

She looked closely at Taylor's dresser. For as much as she didn't seem to care about keeping her kitchen stocked, the opposite was true of the bathroom. The counter was littered with makeup including an open eye shadow case and multiple lipsticks. Two hairbrushes and one comb were shoved in a corner next to a small vial of perfume.

The medicine cabinet was full of over the counter medication like Advil, Benadryl, and Pepto-Bismol, but there were no bottles of prescription drugs. The shower had several quarter-filled bottles of shampoo and conditioner, some facial cleanser, a leg razor, shaving cream, and a bar of conditioning soap.

Jessie stepped out of the bathroom and the strong smell, which had been temporarily masked by the scents in the bathroom, hit her again. She glanced back down the hallway, noting again the complete lack of anything personal on the walls.

"Before we go into the bedroom," she said, turning to Wayne, "let me know how much of this I have right. Taylor Jansen is single, white, attractive and in her late twenties to early thirties. She works close by and travels often. She has few friends. She's extremely detail-oriented. And she has enough money to be living somewhere much nicer than this."

Wayne's eyes went wide briefly before he responded.

"She was thirty exactly," he said. "Birthday was last month. She is white and looks to have been very pretty. She does work close by, at a gym less than a full block from here. We're reconfirming her relationship status. But her co-worker, the one who found her, says she wasn't currently involved. He's downstairs in a black and white giving his statement again if you want to talk to him. I can't speak to the travel and financials but maybe he can."

"We'd love to talk to him as soon as we're done here," Ryan said before turning to Jessie. "You ready to go in?"

She nodded. It wasn't lost on her that with a few exceptions, her description of Taylor Jansen could have been of herself too. She would turn thirty in a few weeks. Her downtown apartment was as Spartan as this one and not because she hadn't had time to decorate it. She could count her good friends on a couple of fingers. And setting aside her recent marriage to a man who had tried to kill her, she was not, despite her conversation with Ryan, currently involved. If she died tomorrow, would another profiler's thumbnail analysis of her be any different than the woman behind that bedroom door?

"You want any?" Wayne asked as he applied some eucalyptus-scented cream just below his nostrils. It helped fight the nasty smells that were about to grow stronger.

"No thanks," Jessie said. "As bad as it is, I need all my senses at full strength when I go to a scene. Blocking out one smell might mask another important one."

"It's your stomach," Wayne said, shrugging as he opened the door.

Almost immediately, Jessie regretted her decision.

CHAPTER FIVE

The stench was overwhelming. The woman must have been dead for last two, maybe three days. She was lying on the bed with the covers off, wearing workout pants and a sports bra. There were no obvious signs of a struggle in how she was positioned or in the room generally. Nothing looked to have been knocked to the floor. Nothing was broken. Her clothing didn't appear to have been disturbed. She had no obvious cuts or marks.

Of course, that didn't prove anything. If this was foul play, the perpetrator would have had lots of time to clean up the room and Taylor before leaving. Fingerprints on items in the room, including the body, might offer some help on that front. But at least visibly, nothing had been disturbed.

Jessie walked over to get a closer look at the victim. The team from the medical examiner's office, who had been about to put her in a body bag, took a respectful step back.

Taylor Jansen's face was blue and puffy. Her eyes were closed. The abdomen she'd clearly worked so hard to keep tight and flat was now distended—a result of the gases that had built up inside her after death. Even in this condition, Jessie could tell that she had been beautiful.

"Has anyone touched her?" Ryan asked.

"Other than to get prints, no," Wayne assured them.

"She looks like she died taking a nap," Ryan noted. "No wonder the initial call was suicide. Maybe not all those pills in the cases in the kitchen were vitamins. I'm very curious to see the toxicology report."

Jessie leaned in close and noted the dull bruises on Taylor's wrists and neck. Because of the skin discoloration and bloating, it was hard to tell how old they were. But if she had to guess, they'd been there well before two days ago.

"Was that window near the front door always open?" Jessie asked. "Or did someone do it after she was found?"

"According to her co-worker, it was slightly open when he arrived. He said he knocked on the door and tried to open it. But it was locked so he used the window to get in."

Jessie nodded, turning away from Taylor's body and walking over to her closet. She pushed open the sliding door and glanced inside. It looked like three-quarters of her wardrobe was comprised exclusively of workout gear and lingerie. She turned back to Ryan and Officer Wayne.

"We definitely need to talk to her co-worker," she said.

Vin Stacey looked miserable sitting in the back of the patrol car parked outside the complex.

"Is he being held?" Jessie asked the bored-looking officer standing beside the car.

"No. We just asked him to stick around until you all could come down and talk to him."

"Does he know he doesn't have to wait in the car? Because he looks like he thinks he's being detained."

"We didn't specifically clarify the nature of our request," the officer admitted sheepishly. "We just asked him to wait in the vehicle for additional questioning."

"So he thinks he's under arrest?" Jessie said incredulously.

"I don't know what impression he has, ma'am. We just made the request."

Jessie looked over at Ryan, who didn't seem anywhere near as irate as she felt.

"You cool with this?" she demanded.

"No," he said. "But I can't deny I've used the tactic before. It's a way of keeping someone around without having to formally arrest him."

"But I thought he wasn't a suspect anymore," Jessie countered.

"Everyone's a suspect. You know that."

"Okay," Jessie conceded. "But meanwhile, he's sitting there with the whole world walking by, thinking he's been arrested for something."

"I guess we should clear that up then," Ryan said flatly.

Jessie frowned at him before opening the back door.

"Mr. Stacey?" she asked, losing the edge she'd just had. Her voice was all honey now.

"Yes," he answered shakily.

"Why don't you come on out of the vehicle? I'm sorry you had to wait so long. My colleague and I were upstairs investigating. We were hoping to ask some follow-up questions, if you don't mind."

"I've answered everybody's questions," he pleaded. "I don't know why I'm in trouble."

"You're not in trouble, Mr. Stacey," she promised. "Come on out. My name is Jessie Hunt. I'm a criminal profiler for the LAPD. This is Detective Ryan Hernandez. I see a coffee shop on the corner there. Let us buy you a cup and we can talk. How would that be?"

He nodded and eased himself out of the vehicle. It was only then that Jessie realized just how massive he was. Standing at his full height, he was easily six foot two. Jessie guessed that he was 220 pounds. He was wearing a form-fitting long-sleeved workout shirt that hugged his prominent abs. His biceps looked like they might rip through the fabric at any moment.

Despite his imposing manner, she sensed gentleness in his bearing. Glancing more closely at him, she noticed that he wore a tight necklace with a rainbow charm and his fingernails were painted a sparkly purple.

"So I'm guessing you're a trainer at Taylor's gym too?" she said, trying to lighten the mood slightly as they walked to the coffee shop.

He nodded but didn't respond. Ryan followed a step behind, clearly sensing that his presence might inhibit her attempts to cultivate a connection with Stacey. As they walked, Jessie noticed the man rubbing his wrists gingerly.

"You okay?" she asked.

"I still can't believe it. I feel like my insides have been scooped out. Waiting there, just knowing that a person who had such a lively spirit was now just this cold, lifeless object only feet away from me. It hurts just to think about it. And your people only made it worse."

"That was unfortunate," Jessie acknowledged.

"Did you know that the officers put me in handcuffs when they got to Taylor's place?" he pressed. "I was just sitting out there, waiting for them. And one of them cuffed me while the other had his hand on his gun holster the whole time. I was the one who called 911!"

"I'm really sorry about that, Mr. Stacey," she soothed. "Unfortunately, when officers first arrive on the scene, they have to take precautions that might seem excessive after the fact."

"They kept me cuffed for a half hour, long after they got my ID, checked to see if I had a record, which I don't, and confirmed that I worked with Taylor. This was all while she's lying dead on her bed. I think we both know that if *you* had called 911 and been waiting there, they would have treated you differently."

"Right," she said, nodding sympathetically as they entered the coffee shop. She looked at the officer who had been trailing for him and indicated for him to stay outside.

"So you worked with her, you said. You were both trainers?" she continued, trying to move on from Stacey's indignation.

"Yeah—at Solstice."

"The gym right across from her apartment?" Jessie asked, remembering the fitness club she'd seen when they arrived.

"Nice commute, right?" he said.

They ordered coffees and sat down at a nearby table. Ryan joined them but didn't speak.

"So before we get into how you found her, Mr. Stacey . . ."

"Call me Vin," he said.

"Okay, Vin," she obliged. "Before that, I want you to tell us about Taylor. What was she like? Friendly? Quiet? Easygoing? Intense?"

"I wouldn't call her easygoing. She was polite but professional with the other trainers and staff. She was warmer with her clients but there was still a very businesslike vibe. That was her thing. Some clients like their trainer to be a chatty best friend. That's kind of my thing. Others want someone who is no nonsense and will help them achieve their goals. She was the go-to person for that."

"What kind of clients did she mostly have?" Ryan asked, speaking for the first time.

Vin looked at Jessie hesitantly, as if he needed her approval to respond. She nodded reassuringly and he went on.

"She had all kinds. But I'd say that over half were married women in their thirties and forties. Lots of wealthy stay-at-home wives trying to lose the baby weight or keep firm enough to prevent their husbands from leaving them for their secretaries."

"That was her bread and butter?" Ryan said.

"Yeah. She was really great at empowering those women and making them feel as if they were in control of their own destinies. I'm a single, gay black man and sometimes she made me want to marry a middle-aged white guy just so I could take charge of my life."

"So were you close?" Jessie asked.

"Not that close," he said. "We'd get coffee—here sometimes actually, or go for a drink. I walked her home a couple of times late at night. But I wouldn't say were friends—more casual work friendly. I think she liked me because I was one of the few men in that club who didn't hit on her all the time."

"Were any of them especially aggressive?" Ryan asked.

"I'm not sure I'm the best judge of what women consider aggressive these days," he admitted. "All I can say is that she never seemed intimidated by any of them. She had no problem shutting a guy down hard if he got out of line."

"Do you know her relationship status?" Jessie asked. "You told the officers upstairs that she wasn't involved."

"I said I didn't *think* she was currently involved. I know she was dating some guy a few months ago. But after it ended she got really secretive about her romantic life. And it wasn't my place to push so I can't claim to be an expert."

"Vin," Jessie asked, deciding to cut to the question she knew they'd be tangling with the rest of the day, "do you think Taylor might have killed herself?"

He responded immediately and with an intensity they hadn't yet seen from him.

"No way. Taylor just wasn't that kind of person. She was driven, focused. She was one of those people who had concrete goals. She wanted to start her own gym. She never would have short-circuited herself. She was what I like to call a marrow sucker."

"What does that mean?" Jessie asked.

"She sucked the marrow out of life. She never would have ended hers."

They all sat quietly for a moment before Ryan returned to a less philosophical topic.

"Do you know the name of her ex?" he asked.

"No. But I think one of the female trainers at the club might. I remember that she said she saw him drop Taylor off once and recognized him."

As Vin answered, Jessie's eyes went to the coffee shop entrance, where a clearly homeless man walked in. He had a long beard and shoes with soles that were so loose they flopped every time he lifted a foot.

That wasn't what caught her attention though. Something red was dripping from the man's left hand and his right hand was hidden under his jacket. He was muttering to himself as he moved among the other customers, seemingly bumping into some of them intentionally.

"What's that trainer's name?" Ryan asked. His back was to the door and he hadn't noticed the man yet.

"Chianti."

"Are you serious?" Ryan asked, laughing involuntarily and spitting up a bit of his coffee.

"I don't know if that's her birth name," Vin said, smiling for the first time. "But at the gym she goes by Chianti Rossellini. It's not my place to judge."

"Why do I think that's not actually your philosophy, Vin?" Jessie said archly as she kept half an eye on the homeless man.

Vin raised his eyebrows provocatively.

"I hate to break this up this gossip session . . ." Ryan said.

"You can do whatever you want, brown eyes," Vin interrupted, batting his own.

Ryan didn't respond to that, instead plowing ahead.

"But we need to ask you about when you found Taylor. You told the officers the window was open?"

Vin's face immediately fell.

"Just a little bit, yes. I knocked first and checked the door, which was locked. But when she didn't respond I opened the window wider and climbed in. I guess I could have called 911 first. But I thought if she was hurt and needed help, I shouldn't just stand there waiting around."

"You don't have to justify yourself, Vin," Jessie said. "You were worried about a friend. I'm sure the evidence will support that."

"Thank you," Vin said, his voice cracking slightly.

Jessie would have had a stronger emotional reaction to him if she wasn't so fixated on the homeless man with the small stream of blood dripping from his arm. He was now rocking back and forth from heel to toe and his right hand was moving under his jacket, which appeared to be damp with a thick liquid.

It looked like he was hitting himself in the hip. His lips were still moving but whatever he was muttering was now inaudible, though the middle-aged woman in line ahead of him kept glancing back nervously.

"Hey, Ryan," she said nonchalantly, "Take a casual look over your left shoulder at the bearded guy in line."

Ryan glanced over, as did Vin.

"The one who can't stop moving his body or his lips?" Ryan asked.

"Yep," Jessie confirmed. "He's bleeding from his left arm and I think he's holding something with his right hand under the jacket."

"What do you think it is?"

"I'm not sure. But I noticed a dark, wet stain in the hip area of the jacket. So I'm assuming it's whatever made his other hand bleed. Also, he seems pretty agitated. He was bumping into other customers and not on accident."

"It could be something," Ryan said quietly. "Or he could be like half the folks we passed on the street on the way over here."

"That's true," Jessie agreed, "though the whole 'blood' thing adds a little drama. Also, all the baristas look terrified and I bet they have homeless folks come in here all the time."

"Fair point," Ryan said, wincing slightly as he stood up. "I think I might get in line for a refill. Jessie, maybe you could quietly grab that officer from outside and ask him to come in as a precaution?"

Jessie nodded and stood up herself, trying to hide the twinge of pain she felt in both her back and her leg after having been immobile for several min-utes. As she moved to the shop entrance, she glanced back over her shoulder and saw that Ryan had taken up a position right behind the mumbling man. She pushed open the front door and waved to the uniformed officer she'd chastised earlier.

"I think we may have a situation in here," she said. "The bearded man standing in front of Detective Hernandez might have a weapon under his jacket. We're not sure but we could use some backup just in case."

She had barely finished her sentence when a loud scream erupted from inside. She turned around to see the middle-aged woman in line clutching her right shoulder with her left hand. Behind her, Ryan was struggling to rip a hunt-ing knife out of the hands of the mumbling man. But despite his size advantage, it was a losing battle.

The other man had a frenzied anger about him and Ryan clearly wasn't at full strength. Within moments, the man had freed himself. Ryan lost his balance and fell to the floor as the man regrouped and lunged at him.

Jessie hurried back inside, unbuttoning her gun holster as she moved toward them. She was just removing her weapon when there was a flash of movement in front of her. It was Vin Stacey, who leapt at the mumbling man, smashing his forearm into the man's jaw and sending him careening back against the counter.

The knife flew out of the dazed man's hand and slid across the floor. Vin stood over him, ready to proceed if necessary. It wasn't. A moment later, the officer was on the man, turning him onto his stomach and cuffing him. Jessie reholstered her gun and knelt down beside Ryan.

"You okay?" she asked urgently.

"Yeah. I'll recover, although I'm not sure my pride will."

Vin walked over and extended his hand.

"Want a little help, brown eyes?" he asked, batting his eyes flirtatiously.

CHAPTER SIX

Jessie's confidence was shaken.

As she and Ryan waited in the lobby of Solstice Health & Fitness while the general manager found Chianti, she kept flashing back to that three-second window before Vin had knocked the homeless man to the ground.

In that brief stretch of time, Ryan had fallen, a man had tried to kill him and Jessie had failed to act quickly enough to prevent it. If not for the quick action of a human tank with fast feet and a bit of a crush, Detective Ryan Hernandez might be dead right now.

Before taking the woman the homeless guy had stabbed to the hospital, one of the EMTs had looked Ryan over and given him the all clear. But Jessie couldn't help but wonder if either of them was really ready to be back in the field yet.

Her internal debate was interrupted when the general manager motioned for them to come onto the fitness floor. As they did, she forced those concerns from her mind, trying to stay focused on the case at hand. As they walked over, Jessie glanced around the gym, trying not to let the pounding house music give her a headache.

The main room was massive, with a seemingly endless array of cardio machines. Off to the left was the weight "room" which was so vast she couldn't even see where it ended. To the right were two dozen mats intended for stretching and, right now at least, for chatting while scrolling through phones.

The GM, a bushy-mustached man named Frank Stroup, stood waiting beside a skinny but ripped blonde woman in her late twenties wearing what Jessie considered far too much makeup for the gym. Her teeth were unnaturally bright and her breasts were squeezed together by a sports bra that looked several sizes too small.

"Detectives," the GM said, forgetting that only one of them had that title, "this is Chianti Rossellini. I'll leave you to your questions. Please let me know if I can be of any more help."

Jessie nodded politely. He hadn't been of much help at all actually. Other than giving the basics on Taylor's employment history, he seemed to know little about her life. The facility may have been huge but Jessie thought it odd that the guy didn't have more to say about a trainer that Vin suggested worked with some of their wealthiest members. They had intentionally avoided mentioning her death to him. But even so, Jessie would have expected him to at least be curious about why she'd been out for the last two days.

As he walked off, Chianti stared at them with a mix of apprehension and curiosity. She seemed to think she was in trouble for something. But her body language suggested she wasn't sure for what.

"Ms. Rossellini," Ryan began, managing not to start giggling mid-sentence, "how well do you know Taylor Jansen?"

"You can call me Chianti," she replied, unaware just how challenging that might be. "I know her some. I mean, we work at the same gym. We interact most days. But I wouldn't say we're friends or anything. Taylor is very focused on her clients and doesn't spend much time on chitchat. What's this about anyway? Has she done something wrong?"

"These are just routine questions. No need for you to concern yourself beyond that," Jessie said, not ready to reveal the truth until it served their purposes. "What can you tell us about her ex-boyfriend, the one who sometimes dropped her off here?"

"Oh, that would be Gavin. Gavin Peck."

"Tell us about Gavin, Chianti," Jessie said conversationally.

"Okay," she said, losing the uneasiness almost immediately. "Gavin is a piece of work. He's built, for sure. I think he's even won a few weight-lifting competitions. And he's—what's the nice way to say it—volatile."

"What do you mean?" Ryan pressed.

"He's just super-intense. I used to work out at the gym he goes to and he was always amped up—really high energy. Taylor is high energy too. But in a more controlled way. He tends to fly off the handle."

"Did he ever fly off the handle with Taylor?" Jessie probed.

"I only saw them together a couple of times and he was never like that with her. But I don't think he took the breakup very well."

"Why do you say that?" Ryan asked, giving Chianti his best "I'm really interested in what you have to say" look. She almost melted right in front of him.

"I heard that he came around a couple of times and security had to ask him to leave," she said, blushing slightly. "I don't know if that's true. But it sounds like Gavin. He's got a stalkerish vibe. Plus, he might have reason to be jealous."

"Of what?" Jessie wanted to know.

"Not to speak out of school or anything, but Taylor can be kind of flirtatious with her clients."

Just then, a pale, paunchy thirty-something guy in a sleeveless gray shirt walked by.

"Hi, Chianti," he said shyly.

"Hey, Brett, we still on for your 11 a.m. session?" she asked, flashing those extra bright teeth.

"Of course."

"Excellent, sweetie. We'll keep those biceps buff, okay? See you soon."

When he left, the smile evaporated and she immediately returned her attention to Jessie.

"Where were we?" she asked.

"You were saying Taylor can be flirtatious," Jessie reminded her with a straight face.

"Right."

"Really?" Jessie pushed. "We heard she's very professional."

"On the workout floor, sure. But I heard her on the phone, making appointments for private training sessions. Management officially frowns on that so she kept it on the down low. But her tone on those calls was definitely less ... professional."

"Do you think she offers more than just training sessions?" Jessie asked leadingly.

"I couldn't say," Chianti replied, shrugging. "I mean, who knows whether she's promiscuous or just a tease. Either way, the managers turned a blind eye because so many of her clients are big spenders. They didn't want to risk losing memberships, you know? But sometimes she didn't come in for days and no one said a word. If I did that, I'd be dumped fast. In fact, I haven't seen her in a while. I figured this was just another one of those times. But now you've got me worried. Is she okay?"

Jessie glanced at Ryan, letting him know she thought the time was right. He nodded in agreement and stepped in close to Chianti.

"I'm afraid she's not," he said quietly. "Taylor is dead."

Jessie watched Chianti closely as she took in the news. The trainer's plastic smile immediately disappeared. She looked disbelieving.

"I'm sorry. What?"

"Taylor Jansen was found dead in her apartment this morning," Ryan said emotionlessly.

Chianti seemed to be processing the information, realizing only now the purpose of all the questions she'd been asked. Her face morphed pretty quickly from shock into something between worry and curiosity.

"Was she murdered? Did Gavin do it?"

There was a lack of empathy in her voice that made Jessie want to punch her. They didn't have to be friends, but couldn't the woman at least fake a moment of sorrow? Unfortunately, in Jessie's experience, her reaction also didn't suggest guilt.

The hungry, gossipy look on her face and her naked desire to know the inside details both suggested she had none of them already. While Ryan was right that everybody is a suspect, Jessie's profiling background suggested strongly to her that Chianti wasn't much of one.

"We don't have information about the cause of death at this time," Ryan said, then added reluctantly, "Did Taylor ever strike you as depressed?"

"Oh wow," Chianti said, her eyes getting wide. "Did she kill herself?"

"Just answer the question please, Ms. Rossellini," Jessie snapped, losing patience.

Chianti looked mildly hurt but after a moment, she answered.

"No," she admitted, sounding let down. "Actually, she always seemed pretty even-keeled to me. I never saw her get too high or too low. I'd be really surprised it turned out she did this to herself."

Jessie tried to hide her own disappointment as well. So far, no one they'd spoken to thought Taylor was a likely candidate to commit suicide. And yet, at least so far, they had no evidence to suggest it was anything else.

"Is there anyone you can think of besides Gavin who might have had animosity toward her—a client maybe?" she asked.

Chianti thought for a moment.

"No one jumps out at me. I didn't pay that close attention. But her reputation was that clients were generally happy with her. Some of that was because she was a good trainer. Some of it might be for those other reasons I mentioned, not to speak ill of the dead."

"No, of course not," Jessie said, the disgust rising in her chest. "Maybe you can wrap up here, Detective Hernandez. I need a bit of air."

She nodded at Chianti and left abruptly, passing Brett as she left the workout floor. He was leaning against a treadmill, waiting for his not-at-all-flirty trainer to finish talking so he could start his session with her.

Jessie stepped out of the gym, onto the grimy, traffic-choked Hollywood street, where she somehow felt less dirty than she had around Chianti.

CHAPTER SEVEN

Jessie tensed up. They were getting close now and she wasn't sure how she'd react.

After leaving Hollywood, they headed back to the station. This time she had insisted on driving. Her sarcastic explanation to Ryan, who usually drove, was that this wasn't *Driving Miss Daisy* and that women were permitted to drive in these parts.

But that wasn't the real reason. She knew that if she drove, she could take a route that passed the house where her recently orphaned stepsister, Hannah Dorsey, was currently living with a foster family. Logically, she knew the chances that the girl would be outside as they drove past were remote. But she had to at least try.

As she drove, she tried to diminish her rising anxiety by actually paying attention to what Ryan was saying. He was commenting on the austere nature of Taylor's apartment.

"It makes much more sense that her place was so empty now," he noted. "If what Chianti said was true, she might have spent days at time at a client's house, whether for legitimate or sketchy reasons. She'd only need to keep the basics at her place. Maybe she just came back one day, looked around at how depressing the place was, and decided to end it."

"Maybe," Jessie considered as she turned right, now only a block from Hannah's foster home. "But she doesn't seem the type. I mean, you never know what someone's dealing with on the inside. But no one mentioned her ever seeming depressed. I think the toxicology report will be determinative."

"In the interim, we could check with her family for a history of depression or anything else," Ryan suggested.

"It's worth a shot," Jessie said. "But while the EMT at the coffee shop was checking you out, I talked to Vin a bit more. He mentioned that she didn't have any family in the area and that they were estranged anyway. I guess that soup in the freezer from her mother was an unsuccessful peace offering. I'm not sure how much insight they'll be able to give us. I think the suicide idea is a red herring."

"How can you be so sure?" he asked.

"I'm not sure. But don't you find it suspicious that there was no note or any indication that she was depressed? Or that her window was open?"

"Maybe she liked to keep her place cool after getting home from the gym," Ryan offered. "It's a lot cheaper than using the air-conditioning."

Jessie glanced over at him and could tell that even he didn't buy the theory.

"Regardless," he continued, not acknowledging her skepticism, "Hollywood Division is sending us copies of all the evidence they collected. We can go through her client list and see if anyone pops."

"How did the Hollywood detectives feel about us bigfooting them?" Jessie asked.

"Pretty much as resentful as you'd expect," he said. "But I was cryptic, said the case might be connected to an ongoing investigation. They didn't want to risk playing hardball if it meant interfering in something major, so they backed down. Everything should be waiting for us at the station when we get back."

"Sounds good," Jessie said, noting the tightness in her throat. She had just turned onto Hannah's street.

She slowed down to the posted speed limit, happy to use the speed bumps on the road as an excuse. The house was on the left, an unremarkable ranch style home. The front porch had a hammock that was currently unoccupied, which made perfect sense at lunchtime on a weekday. Still, she felt let down.

She didn't know what she had expected. Even if Hannah had been there, what would she have done? She was expressly prohibited from initiating any contact with the girl by Children's Family Services, Captain Decker, and, more informally, by her own therapist, Dr. Janice Lemmon.

It was a reasonable request. Only eight weeks ago, the only family the girl had ever known had been slaughtered before her eyes. That was more than enough for any seventeen-year-old to deal with. But how would she handle learning that the man who did it was her birth father? And that the woman who he had tortured within an inch of her life was her half-sister?

Of course, no one could be expected to download all that horror and still function. Was she supposed to just compartmentalize those facts by focusing on studying for her pre-calculus test or finishing *Moby Dick*? It was crazy to want to engage her.

And yet, Jessie felt a deep yearning to do exactly that. She pushed down the desire as they passed the house. Ryan, who had no clue about its significance, or even that she had a half-sister, seemed oblivious, which she took as a sign that she was doing a solid job of faking it. As she turned onto the next street, she flashed back to her most recent therapy session with Dr. Lemmon, trying to remind herself of what the woman had said.

Janice Lemmon knew what she was talking about and was not someone to be disregarded lightly. Well into her sixties, she might not look imposing with her thick glasses and tight blonde perm. But in addition to being a highly regarded behavioral therapist, she was also a legendary criminal profiler who still occasionally consulted on cases for the LAPD, FBI and other organizations that required top secret security clearance.

It was Lemmon who had connected Jessie, then a married graduate student, with the criminology professor who got her access to Bolton Crutchfield while he was incarcerated. It was Lemmon who put in the word that got Jessie the provisional profiler position with the department.

And while both Decker and Hernandez gave recommendations, she was also instrumental in Jessie being accepted to the ten-week training program she'd recently taken at the FBI Academy in Quantico, Virginia, where she studied at the famed Behavioral Sciences unit and underwent intense physical training that included weapons instruction and self-defense classes.

Janice Lemmon's opinion was to be taken seriously and Jessie tried to remind herself of that. As they sat in her comfy office on deep-set leather chairs, the doctor, in her calm, understated voice, asked Jessie what she thought it would do to Hannah's psyche to deal with all the information currently being held from her.

"It would make her brain melt," Jessie admitted.

"Not just her brain, but her soul too, Jessie," Dr. Lemmon said. "You are a full-grown adult who deals with murderers and serial killers for a living. And you're barely holding on. Imagine how a girl with no experience or coping tools would handle this kind of knowledge. She'd emotionally disintegrate."

"I know," Jessie said reluctantly.

"Listen," Dr. Lemmon continued. "I get it. Just like her, your adoptive parents were taken from you, by the same person in fact. He murdered your mother. Your family is gone, or so you thought. And now you learn that you have this person who shares part of your DNA and your personal history. It makes perfect sense that you would want to connect with her. And in time, it might make sense to do so. But not right now. It wouldn't help her. And if you think about it clearly, you'll realize that it won't actually help you either. You have to be patient, Jessie."

Patience.

As she turned onto 6th Street, which was a straight shot to the station, Jessie silently acknowledged that patience was not her strongest attribute. And yet, if she was ever going to create some kind of meaningful relationship with her only remaining relative, she'd have to try.

Of course, if she was honest, reconnecting with family wasn't the only reason she wanted to talk to Hannah again. There was another, darker reason, one she was hesitant to say out loud, even to Dr. Lemmon.

Back at the height of their cat and mouse game, Xander Thurman sent Jessie a video asking her to join him on his murderous spree. He insisted they were the same and that together they could cleanse the world. She rejected his offer, which led him to declare she was unsalvageable and had to be killed.

But even though she had been appalled by the very suggestion that she might be like the man who had killed her mother, her adoptive parents and dozens of other people, the seed had been planted. Some part of her wondered if there was any truth to the claim.

Could she, simply by virtue of being his daughter and sharing his blood, also share his sickness too? Was that why she was drawn to this work, in which she was constantly surrounded by death and murder and people not unlike her own father?

She told herself that she'd picked this profession because she'd seen evil up close, because she literally knew its face, and was therefore more equipped to battle it better than most others. But was that the only reason?

Was there some part of her that did this job because it allowed her to be close to violence and cruelty but mask the thrill under the guise of fighting those things? There were days she wasn't entirely sure she didn't have the same infection as her dad.

And on those days, she couldn't help but wonder the same thing about Hannah. Was there any part of the girl that was drawn to the darkness that defined her father? Was she just a normal teenage girl or had she exhibited any signs that there might be something else going on beneath the surface?

Jessie felt guilty even asking the question, as if she was denying a girl she didn't even know the benefit of the doubt that she was a decent person. And yet that doubt lingered in her mind.

Of course, there wasn't much she could do. She couldn't talk to Hannah to glean anything about her character. And doing any kind of probing into her life or background was sure to raise immediate red flags with Decker, who had been very clear that the girl was off-limits in every way.

I can't do anything about it.

As she pulled into the Central Station parking garage, the germ of a terrible, brilliant idea occurred to her. Perhaps *she* couldn't pursue the matter, but that didn't mean it couldn't be pursued. There was no reason someone else couldn't look into Hannah's background to see if there were any red flags there. And she knew of the exact person who might be able to pursue it.

Chapter Eight

The solution had been in front of her the whole time. But for some reason, she hadn't been able to see it until now.

Her friend Kat Gentry was one of the few people, along with Captain Decker and an FBI agent named Dolan, who knew that Jessie and Hannah were related. She'd been in the hospital room with Jessie when she'd learned the news.

But Kat was also a highly decorated former Army Ranger who had served two tours in Afghanistan and had the shrapnel burn scars on her face and body to prove it. After she returned stateside, she worked in security, which ultimately led to a position as head of security at the lockdown facility where Bolton Crutchfield was held.

Unfortunately for her, once he escaped with the help of a rogue guard, she was fired. After taking several months off to deal with the guilt she undeservedly placed on herself, she decided to take up a new, but related line of work. She became a private detective.

To Jessie, it seemed like a perfect fit. She could go to someone she implicitly trusted to investigate her half-sister, someone she knew wouldn't reveal her family secret, because she already knew it. Kat would be discreet, out of both friendship and to prove her mettle as a detective. It would also allow Jessie to throw some work to a loyal friend in need.

Of course, if it got back to Decker that Kat was investigating Hannah, he'd know that Jessie was somehow involved. But he wouldn't be able to easily prove it. And that one degree of separation should be enough to protect her professionally.

As she and Ryan walked into the station, Jessie felt like a weight had been lifted from her. She could finally get some answers via a trusted source who wouldn't betray her. That was a rarity these days. She felt bad that she couldn't tell Ryan about the plan. But by keeping him in the dark, she was actually protecting him.

When they returned to the bullpen, the room was still half empty. They walked over to their desks to find the only HSS detective around was Alan Trembley, who, at twenty-nine, was the junior member of the unit.

"What's the status on the shootout?" Ryan asked him.

"It's a mess, man. We're up to eight dead and another seventeen injured. Most of the team is still on the scene or following up associated leads. I'm only here to check on how things are going with the crime scene samples. I'm heading back out in a few minutes."

"Do you need help?" Ryan asked.

"Of course," Trembley answered. "Even with everyone out there, we're still short on manpower. But there's no point in asking Decker. He was clear that you couldn't get involved. And to be honest, man, it's rough out there. Rounding up some of these gangbangers has been a daunting process. A few of them have resisted pretty aggressively."

"You don't think I'm up for it?" Ryan demanded, offended.

"*I'm* barely up for it, Hernandez. And I wasn't stabbed twice two months ago. I can't believe I'm about to say this but Decker is right. Ease in, man."

"Ease in, he says," Ryan said, turning to Jessie for support.

"Hey, I'm right there with you," she lied. "But it looks like that evidence file we asked Hollywood station for arrived. Check out your desk."

Ryan glanced down and saw thick manila folder marked with the Hollywood station logo. The fight seemed to drain out of him.

"I guess we're stuck here," he said resignedly.

"Hey, buck up, Hernandez," Trembley offered sarcastically. "Maybe your victim was killed by a gangbanger too. Then you can get in on the action."

Hernandez looked at him disdainfully.

"Didn't you say you had to go?" he asked.

Trembley took the hint and headed off to the CSU lab, leaving Jessie to deal with Ryan's bad mood alone. She grabbed the file and opened it, letting him cool down without worrying that she was watching him. It didn't take long for her to legitimately forget about him.

Only a few pages into the paperwork, she came across a police report. It described a disturbance in the parking garage of Taylor Jansen's complex.

Apparently Gavin Peck had accosted her eleven weeks ago as she was approaching her car to go out for the evening.

They got into an intense argument and the garage attendant had called the police. The arriving officers filed a report and asked Taylor if she wanted to press charges or file for a restraining order. She declined, telling them she was confident there wouldn't be a recurrence of this kind of incident. Neither she nor Peck would reveal the nature of their argument.

It wasn't much to go on but it did reinforce the notion that Gavin Peck had an anger problem. So too did his arrest record, which showed no major incidents but did note two arrests. One was for a bar fight seven years ago. The second was also for fighting, this time in the stands at a Dodgers game four years ago. Considering that he was only thirty-two, he had already built a considerable reputation as a hothead.

Jessie recalled the bruises on Taylor's neck and wrists. They looked old. Could they have been from this parking garage incident or a subsequent one? Between Chianti's statement and the police report, they seemed to have more than enough justification to go have a chat with Gavin.

She passed the police report over to Ryan, who seemed to have calmed down and was now sitting at his desk. As he looked it over, she skimmed through some of the additional paperwork. She stopped when she came to an 8x10 photo of Taylor Jansen that looked like it had been taken professionally, maybe for her work as a trainer.

This was the first time Jessie had seen what Taylor looked like alive. Unlike the pale puffy-faced woman they'd found on the bed, the woman staring back at her was vibrant and beautiful. Her brown hair was pulled back in a ponytail, so as not to hide her sculpted cheekbones and long, toned neck. Her eyes were brown too and held a focused intensity. Her lips hinted at a smile.

It was clear why clients might be drawn to her. She was stunning, but in a tough, no-nonsense way that suggested she didn't care that much about how she looked. She projected competence and confidence, traits that anyone looking for a personal trainer would seek out, regardless of her looks.

And though Jessie was hesitant to draw any definitive conclusions based solely on her interpretation of a photo, there was something about Taylor's set jaw line that implied she was unlikely to take crap from anyone, including a boyfriend, current or ex. She looked like someone who liked to be in control.

"I guess we're paying Gavin Peck a visit," Ryan said, interrupting her thoughts.

"I guess so," she agreed, putting down the photo. "Maybe we should update Decker before we head out."

"You know he's going to push us to focus on the suicide angle," Ryan groaned.

"That's fine," she reminded him. "But until the toxicology report says that definitively, he can't oppose us pursuing other leads, like, say, a potential stalker ex-boyfriend. We're just doing our due diligence."

"You make it sound so matter-of-fact," he said, impressed.

"You can do it too, Ryan," she said. "I've seen it. You're just out of practice. The less anxious you seem to go out and chase suspects, the more likely the captain is to loosen up. Just act like you're fine working this case. Your restlessness is what's making him nervous. Frankly, it's making me a bit nervous too."

He gave her a faux offended look that she suspected masked some real hurt feelings. Deciding to let him work through that on his own, she grabbed the file and headed to Decker's office. Ryan may have viewed this case as a loser. But she didn't. The woman in that photo was counting on her to uncover the truth and she intended to do it.

She knocked on the already open door.

"What?" Decker barked.

"We wanted to update you on next steps in the Jansen case," she said.

"I thought that was ruled a suicide."

"Not yet," answered Ryan, who had just joined her, his eyebrows raised in "I told you so" mode. "We're still waiting on the preliminary toxicology report and there are some major question marks."

"Like what?" Decker asked, waving them into the office impatiently.

Jessie jumped in, not wanting Ryan to look too anxious to sell the case.

"Like old bruises on her wrists and neck; like an ex-boyfriend with a history of violence; like no one we spoke to thinking she was capable of suicide."

"People can be oblivious to the signs," Decker said in a tone that made Jessie think he knew more about that topic than the average person.

"Of course, Captain," she agreed gently. "And it's still very possible. But until we get something definitive from the medical examiner, it seems to wise to run this other stuff down. We were planning to pay a visit to the ex-boyfriend next."

"That's a good call," he acknowledged. "But here's my concern. I heard about the little coffee shop dustup this morning. Were you going to mention that, Hernandez?"

"It was nothing, sir," Ryan said, trying to sound nonchalant. "An unstable homeless man got a little raucous inside the place. One woman was slightly injured but that was it."

"My understanding is that you had to get checked out by the EMTs."

"It was precautionary, sir. I ended up on the ground in the hubbub," Ryan said, in full downplay mode.

"Is that your recollection of the incident, Hunt?" Decker asked skeptically.

"I was getting the uniformed officer from outside," she said, trying not to sound evasive. "By the time we got inside, the action was pretty much over."

Decker was quiet for several seconds before replying. When he did speak it was slowly and with emphasis."

"You are not cleared for fieldwork. The only reason you're on this case is because we're so short-handed due to the gang shooting. Going to see an ex-boyfriend who is a potential murder suspect is an inherently risky proposition. I want you to bring two officers with you. That's not negotiable. Are we clear?"

"Of course, Captain," Ryan said reassuringly, giving Jessie a half-glance. "We'll absolutely do that. And I know you're just doing your own due diligence. But I promise, we're good to go."

Jessie nodded in agreement. But the truth was, she wasn't so sure.

Chapter Nine

Jessie was annoyed with herself.

Her training had taught her to avoid assumptions but they sometimes leaked in anyway. She had figured Gavin Peck's place would be similar to Jessie's—a sterile apartment in a nondescript complex. But to her surprise, the address they pulled up to was a charming, if small, one-story house sandwiched in between two much larger homes in the Beachwood Canyon section of the Hollywood Hills.

They got out, as did the officers who arrived with them, and walked up the path to his front door. One officer took up a position near the side gate, where he could watch the front door and the backyard. The other stood beside Ryan and Jessie, who knocked on the door.

"Mr. Peck," she said in a loud but hopefully unthreatening voice, "this is the Los Angeles Police Department. May we have a word with you, please?"

She unsnapped her holster but kept her hand off, letting it rest casually but still closely beside her weapon. Ryan did the same but the officer with them had his hand on his sidearm, ready to remove it at a moment's notice. After several seconds without a response, Jessie tried again.

"Gavin Peck," she said in a not-quite-shout as she rapped on the door harder, "this is the LAPD. We need to ask you a few questions. Please come to the door."

"Should we bust it in?" the gangly, overly enthusiastic officer with them asked.

Ryan looked at his name tag for the first time before responding.

"Based on what, Officer Dooley?" he asked. "There's no imminent threat to us or sign of illegal behavior in or near the home. He's not a formal suspect in any crime. And we don't have a warrant. Are you aware of some exigent circumstances that the rest of aren't?"

Jessie thought he was a bit harsh but agreed with the general assessment.

"No sir," Dooley said, chastened.

"Okay then," Ryan said, softening slightly. "We looked up his car and it doesn't appear to be here. It's the middle of the day. It's possible the guy is at work. We don't have a warrant. So we may just have to try something else."

"You looking for Pecker?" someone shouted from behind them.

Everyone whirled around. Dooley unholstered his weapon as he turned and began to raise it in the direction of the voice before Ryan put his hand on the young officer's forearm and quietly whispered, "Easy."

They found themselves looking at a sixty-something man on the sidewalk with his dog. He had on slacks with a white T-shirt that said simply "The Corps." He wore a baseball with "USMC" emblazoned on the front.

"Don't shoot," he said, sounding surprisingly unconcerned. "My VA benefits might not cover it."

"Sorry about that, sir," Ryan said quickly. "We're looking for Gavin Peck. Do you know him?"

"I do. I just call him Pecker though," he said, then looked at Jessie. "Excuse me, ma'am."

"That's okay," she replied. "Is that because he's a jerk?"

"Nah. I just like to tease him. Gussy and I sometimes pass him on our walks when he's out for a run. I'll give him a hard time, shout stuff like 'You got it, Pecker,' 'Run, Pecker, run.' He loves it."

"I'm sure he does," Jessie agreed. "Do you know where Pecker is now, sir?"

"He works from home, but I know he likes to get in a midday workout sometimes."

"Do you happen to know where he works out?" Jessie asked.

"Some meathead gym in Hollywood on La Brea—I can't remember the name. Is Pecker in some kind of trouble?"

"What makes you say that?" Ryan asked. "Does he get in a lot of trouble?"

"Not that I know of," the man said. "It's just that—with the multiple officers and the weapons being pulled out and the banging on the door—this doesn't feel like a social call."

"We're just following up on a lead, sir," Jessie assured him. "Do you mind if we get your contact info in case we have questions down the line?"

"Not a problem, miss. Anything for the boys and girls in blue. I'm Staff Sergeant Joseph Tierney, retired of course."

"Army, right, Staff Sergeant?" Jessie asked playfully.

"Do not insult my honor, young lady," Tierney replied, clearly entertained. "Those are fighting words."

"Apologies, sir," she said with mock over-politeness. "I didn't mean to offend you or Gussy. Officer Dooley, can you please get Mr. Tierney's info? And try not to shoot him."

"It has to be unofficial," Jessie reiterated. "If I'm able to be connected to this in any way, it could cost me more than my job. It could ruin my credibility."

"Don't worry," Kat assured her, her voice a bit staticky over the payphone line. "I'll take the heat if it comes out. My reputation's already shot anyway."

"Thanks, Kat. I owe you."

"Oh, you do owe me," Kat agreed. "In cash. We'll settle up when it's done. For now, just know I'm on it. You focus on the job in front of you, deal?"

"Deal," Jessie said and hung up the payphone. As she walked back down the block to join Ryan for lunch, she was uncertain if what she'd just done might cost her her career.

The wheels were in motion but it wasn't too late to call the whole thing off. She had contacted Kat on her burner cell using a payphone. No harm had been done yet. It was only once Kat started investigating Hannah Dorsey's personal history that they would reach the point of no return. But Jessie didn't want to return.

She had to know more about the girl who shared her blood. At some point they were going to meet and she needed to be prepared. Had Hannah led a conventional teenage life? Or were there any signs that she was somehow genetically corrupted by the father they shared?

When she got back, she found Ryan still in line on the sidewalk. She was starting to think Pink's was a mistake. Yes, the chili dogs were legendary. But the place was a tourist trap with a twenty-minute wait just to place an order.

Still, Ryan had suggested they go, since they were so close. He was hankering for an El Cucuy—a dog with grilled onions, jalapeños and bacon. Jessie found the idea of consuming that before going back to work distasteful bordering on nauseating. She was getting a plain turkey dog, much to Ryan's derision.

"Still waiting on the warrant for Gavin Peck's phone records," he told her when she rejoined him. "But they think they know the gym based on Joe Tierney's description. There's a place called Bulldog Gym that's popular with the power-lifting crowd on La Brea just south of Hollywood Boulevard. We can go there after lunch."

"I'll be curious to see just how much of a meathead this guy is," Jessie said. "I wouldn't have pegged Taylor to be into that kind of guy."

"Shelly used to accuse me of being a meathead sometimes. At the time I thought it was affectionate. But looking back, maybe not so much."

Jessie glanced sideways at him.

"How's all that going?" she asked hesitantly.

"Okay, I guess," he said flatly. "We both want the legal stuff to all be over as quickly as possible so we're trying to keep disagreements to a minimum. Even though I always wanted kids, it's a good thing we didn't have them. That would have made it all so much harder."

"Yeah," Jessie agreed. "That was the one saving grace in my divorce too."

Ryan looked at her with a mix of incredulity and awe.

"You know, I can't believe I'm actually complaining," he said apologetically. "My wife and I drifted apart. Your husband was a literal psychopath who tried to frame you for murdering his mistress and then tried to kill you when you caught him."

"First of all, I'd characterize him more as a sociopath," Jessie jokingly reminded him. "And second, yes, that complicated things. But in the end, I got everything in the split. Plus I don't have to worry about having embarrassing run-ins with him at the supermarket."

"Because he's incarcerated," Ryan noted.

"That's correct."

They both laughed before Ryan took a deep breath. Jessie could sense he wasn't about to crack another joke.

"I have to tell you something," he said, much more quietly than before.

"Okay..."

"I wasn't totally forthcoming this morning when I was explaining why I didn't reach out much while we were both on leave. The truth is ... I felt weird about it."

"Why?" Jessie asked, both afraid and desperate to know.

"I felt guilty. I thought that reaching out to connect to you was in some way a betrayal of my marriage, of all those years spent together. Even though I hadn't done anything wrong, it seemed like making any kind of overture to you was an admission that I was truly, finally giving up on Shelly. But the truth is, she gave up a while ago. It just took me a while to see it. Pretty pathetic huh, considering I'm a detective and all."

Jessie wasn't sure how to respond to all that so instead she just took his hand and squeezed it tightly. He squeezed back. Just then, his cell phone rang. He looked at it.

"It's the medical examiner," he said, hitting speaker. "Go ahead, Lorne. I'm here with Jessie Hunt."

"Hey, guys," Lorne said. "The final toxicology report isn't ready yet. But I have some preliminary results I thought you might find interesting. You ready?"

"Go for it," Ryan said, ignoring the disgruntled look of the woman in line behind them.

"Okay, first thing. It looks like this woman subsisted primarily on protein shakes. I found barely anything in her of nutritive value other than that. Second, we can confirm that she did have some kind of sedative in her system. It's too early to know exactly what or determine quantity."

"Could it have been enough to kill her?" Jessie asked.

"Unlikely," Lorne answered. "It doesn't look like it was that excessive. More than you might typically take before bed but significantly less than someone attempting suicide would use. It would have slowed her heart rate a fair bit though. That's making it hard to determine an accurate time of death. Right now, we're approximating thirty-six to sixty hours ago."

"That would put it sometime between early Monday morning and late Tuesday night," Ryan calculated.

"But we know she wasn't at work on Tuesday," Jessie added. "So it was probably earlier rather than later."

"There's one more thing," Lorne piped in. "She was very early on—only about seven weeks. But Taylor Jansen was pregnant."

CHAPTER TEN

They got their hot dogs to go.

Jessie and Ryan agreed that this new information changed things and to hold off on the Gavin Peck interview until they knew more. On the drive back to the station they got another call, this one from the tech team, which had been able get Taylor's call and text history from the cell phone company. Apparently it was a treasure trove, but one that they'd need to review at the office rather than on the road.

"I wouldn't tell Decker this," Ryan said as Jessie pulled onto Wall Street. "But I still think suicide is on the table."

"Why do you say that?" Jessie asked, rolling down her window all the way. The smell of onions and jalapeños was making her queasy. She had agreed to drive so that he could focus on his dog and finish the thing quickly. But he was taking his sweet, disgusting time.

"I could see her finding out she was pregnant and, in a moment of anxiety, throwing some extra sleeping pills in her protein shake and downing it. Who knows—maybe she thought that would induce a miscarriage."

Jessie stared straight ahead, pondering but not responding.

"You seem skeptical," Ryan finally said.

"A little bit," she admitted. "I'm not ruling it out. But it doesn't seem to fit. I don't claim to have a definitive profile of this woman yet. But based on what I do know, she strikes me as way too assertive to go that route. I see her potentially terminating the pregnancy or deciding to have the baby on her own. But ending her life doesn't add up for me. Maybe inducing a miscarriage but even that seems like a stretch. I think there's another possibility."

"What's that?" he asked, finally, blessedly taking the last bite of his dog.

"What if she told the father she was pregnant and he wasn't overjoyed? Anyone who knew her routine and got access to her place could easily crush up some pills and put it in her protein powder for the day."

"Reasonable theory," he agreed. "Are you thinking Gavin?"

"According to Vin, they broke up months ago and this was pretty recent," Jessie reminded him.

"Maybe they got back together or had a one-night thing," Ryan suggested.

"Or maybe she had a new guy," Jessie countered as she pulled into the station garage.

"All the more reason to check out those phone records," Ryan said.

The treasure trove of records quickly turned into drudgery.

They had decided to go back four months, to one full month before Taylor broke up with Gavin, and work up to the most recent calls and texts. Most of the material was pretty dry. There were lots of conversations about training sessions and nutrition recommendations but very little in the way of personal details. Vin Stacey was right. Taylor didn't seem to have many friends.

Even her breakup communications with Gavin felt businesslike, at least on her end. He seemed rawer about it. Right after the initial breakup, Gavin sent one long thread of messages over the course of an hour. He initially begged her to reconsider, then asked her to at least meet with him, then got upset when she didn't respond and finally said she was making a big mistake that she "will always regret."

It wasn't quite a threat. And about twenty minutes after that message, he sent another one apologizing and saying he'd let his emotions get the better of him. After that, there were no overt threats via text and his calls afterward didn't seem excessive. It would be hard to draw any kind of stalker assumptions based solely on their electronic communications.

Everything seemed back to normal on Taylor's end, with one weird exception. Some of her text communications with one client just didn't make much sense. The client was a married woman named Meadow Horsley, who seemed to have trained with Taylor for at least a year. But starting around two months ago, their texts got very confusing.

They went from the standard confirmations of training appointments, suggestions for workout gear and caloric intake updates to non sequiturs like "you know it," "be there soon," and "now." It was almost as if the comments were in response to messages not sent via text or call.

"Does Taylor have any social media accounts?' she asked Ryan, whose head was in his hands as he pored over Taylor's financials.

He looked up, bleary-eyed.

"I know she has professional Facebook, Instagram and Twitter accounts. They're relentlessly boring."

"What about private messaging on Facebook or direct messages on Twitter?" she asked. "Have we looked at those?"

"I haven't."

"I think she may be using one of them to communicate with one of her clients. Her texts with a woman named Meadow Horsley are a little hinky."

"Okay, let's check it out," Ryan said. "Why don't I take Facebook? You try Twitter. Let's see what we can find."

It didn't take long. According to Ryan, there was nothing unusual in her Facebook private messages. But her Twitter DMs were another story.

"You have to look at this," Jessie said, waving him over to her screen.

When he did, he seemed just as surprised as she was. Up until two months ago, Taylor's messages were fairly innocuous private extensions of public comments on the platform. But around that time they became much more graphic.

It appeared that Taylor's professional relationship with Meadow Horsley had become significantly more intimate. Photos had been taken. Vivid descriptions of what one would do to the other were provided.

As Jessie went through the time and date stamps, it became clear that many of the more explicit Twitter communications matched up with the more mundane texts. So a DM from Meadow saying she was lying naked on her bed waiting was met with a text from Taylor saying, "Be there soon."

Merging the two sets of messages, a picture of a torrid affair emerged. It had gone on unabated until two days ago, when the communication on Taylor's part ended abruptly. Her last message was from Monday morning at 6:17 a.m., saying "have to push next session until Wednesday. New client this morning at 6:30. Sorry for short notice."

Meadow replied via text saying "Understand. Reschedule for Wednesday at 6:30?" But on Twitter she added "Maybe a more personal session can be arranged for later today?"

Taylor never responded to either of those, nor to the Twitter DM a few hours later asking if Taylor wanted to meet her for a lunch break, saying she was in the mood to "eat out." There was no communication the rest of the day. On Tuesday—yesterday—there was one DM from Meadow saying, "Let me know when I can do you ... er, I mean see you." No response.

Today began with a text message from Meadow at 6:15 a.m. that read, "Headed to the gym. We still on for 6:30?" The next one, at 6:37, said, "Where are you?" It was matched by a DM one minute later asking the same thing. She actually called Taylor a minute later but didn't leave a voicemail. At 7:03, Meadow sent a DM asking, "Is something wrong? Are you upset with me?" That was followed by one final text at 7:12 a.m. that said simply "unprofessional." That was over six hours ago. She hadn't communicated since.

When they finished reading the messages, Jessie and Ryan looked up at each other.

"Where does Meadow Horsley live?' he asked.

"Los Feliz."

"Then I guess we're going to Los Feliz."

CHAPTER ELEVEN

Jessie felt queasy.

She wasn't sure if it was due to the lingering scent of Ryan's hot dog in the car or her realization that Taylor's seemingly cut-and-dried life was infinitely more complicated than she'd first thought. It was probably a little bit of both. Either way, her first day back on the job with a seemingly straightforward case was getting messy fast and it was tying her stomach in knots.

As Ryan made the drive to the ritzy Los Feliz neighborhood, she reviewed the information she could find on Meadow Horsley and her husband, Callum.

"So it seems like these are exactly the kinds of people Captain Decker would prefer we not alienate," she said resignedly.

"How's that?" Ryan asked.

"It looks like these two ought to be nominated for sainthood."

"You know I'm inherently suspicious of people who do good works, right?" Ryan said.

"Well then you are going to have serious problems with the Horsleys. According to the website of his hospital, Callum, or 'Cal, as he prefers to be called, is a pediatric cardiologist at Youth Hospital Los Angeles. He is regarded as one of the preeminent heart surgeons in California and has performed lifesaving surgery on over 2,000 children in his decade at YHLA."

"He's overcompensating for something," Ryan said drily.

"Almost certainly," Jessie agreed sarcastically. "Would you like to hear about his equally unimpressive wife, Meadow?"

"I would."

"Well, I'm referring to the same website because she also works at YHLA, where she serves as the Fundraising Administrator. In her eight years there, she has raised over 300 million dollars for the hospital and its services. Prior to that, she held a similar position at the Los Angeles Regional Food Bank. And she does all that in addition to her busy schedule sleeping with and sending risqué selfies to her personal trainer."

"Why are we going to their house then?" Ryan asked. "It sounds like they're more likely to be at the hospital."

"I called their offices already. Both of them took the afternoon off. According to Meadow's assistant they have a couple's massage at their house most Wednesday afternoons. I also had tech run the GPS on their phones so we could test Meadow's alibi for the time of death. Both their phones are at the house right now."

"You know," Ryan said, as he veered right off Western Avenue near the American Film Institute onto Los Feliz Boulevard, which ran just south of Griffith Park, "for a profiler, you sure do a lot of detective work."

"Don't get used to it, Hernandez," she said snarkily. "I'm only helping out because you don't have a partner on this case. Also, because you're out of practice. Basically, I'm covering your ass."

"Much appreciated," he replied, not quipping back.

She tried not to make much of his lack of playfulness. Instead she resumed her report on the couple.

"They've been married for fourteen years. No children of their own. They moved here from Atlanta sixteen years ago. That's where Cal did his residency. They originally lived in Mid-city for five years before buying this place. Financials show they bought the house for 2.4 million. My back of the envelope math suggests that combined, they rake in a little over 1.3 million a year."

"Doing God's work has its benefits," Ryan noted.

Jessie nodded as she focused her attention on the neighborhood, trying to glean as much as she could about the Horsleys from where they chose to live. Even though this section of the resurgent Los Feliz neighborhood was only a mile north of some of the seedier streets of Hollywood, it felt a world away.

It ran along the southern edge of Griffith Park, one of the largest municipal parks in the country, which housed the city zoo, two golf courses, and the famed observatory. But it also contained hundreds of houses, many of which were worth several million dollars.

The Horsleys lived on a cul-de-sac on a hill overlooking the city with an unobstructed view of the downtown skyline. The entire street only had seven homes, all impressive. The Horsley house was a gated two-story Tudor-style mansion. The gate was currently open so Ryan pulled in and parked behind another car in the circular driveway.

As they pulled up, Jessie saw that the front door was open. Two people holding massage tables were stepping outside, accompanied by an auburn-haired, brown-eyed woman in her early forties. Jessie knew it was Meadow from her pictures, which didn't do her justice.

In the website photos she appeared perky and cute. But in person, Meadow Horsley had an extra level of vibrancy that edged into beautiful. She couldn't have been much more than five feet tall, but perhaps because of her aura of palpable energy, she actually looked taller. She almost seemed to be bouncing as she stood waving at the leaving massage therapists. Whatever skin regimen she was using to make her skin glow, Jessie wanted it. And though she was officially middle-aged, the woman had the build of a teenage gymnast, which Jessie suspected she likely was at some point. Her sleeveless form-fitting top and leggings showed toned arms and thighs muscled to the point of near-scariness.

She looked at Jessie and Ryan warily as they exited the car. The massage therapists hesitated, unsure if they should leave her in the company of two strangers. Jessie tried to short-circuit the discomfort.

"Mrs. Horsley, my name is Jessie Hunt. This is Ryan Hernandez. We're investigating a case for the police department. We were hoping you could spare a couple of minutes to help us with a few questions we have."

Meadow Horsley looked briefly taken aback, then motioned for the massage therapists to leave.

"It's okay, Magda. You and Ranya can leave. Just make sure Cal and I are on the schedule for next week."

"Yes, Mrs. H.," Magda said in a thick eastern European accent. "You sure you are okay?"

"It's fine. I'm sure whatever this is about, I can handle it on my own. You two take care."

Magda and Ranya put their tables in the backseat, both scowling at Jessie and Ryan animatedly. When they pulled out, Jessie walked over to Meadow Horsley, who extended her hand.

"Don't mind them," she said. "They're just protective."

"Of what?" Ryan asked, apparently not trying to ingratiate himself.

"Of someone they've helped for six years. Also, we tip well."

Ryan half-grinned at her honesty, despite his best efforts not to.

Please come in," she said, waving them inside. "You can tell me how I can be of service to the . . . who are you with again?"

"LAPD," Jessie said. "Detective Hernandez and I work out of Central Station downtown."

"You're partners?" Horsley asked, leading them down a long hallway to the living room.

"No. I'm a profiler. I consult on cases for the department and I'm helping out here."

"So, you're like that *Silence of the Lambs* girl, Clarice?" she asked as she sat down on one couch and motioned for them to sit on another. "Do you hunt serial killers?"

"Clarice Starling worked for the FBI," Jessie said, intentionally not addressing the specific question as she sat. "But I'm flattered by the comparison. We're here about something far more run of the mill—your personal trainer."

"Our trainer?" Horsley asked, surprised. "You mean Taylor?"

"Yes," Ryan volunteered. "But excuse me—did you say 'our'?"

"Yes," she replied. "Taylor trains both me and my husband, Cal, though he doesn't get in to see her nearly as often as I do. Sometimes we have her come to the house to accommodate his schedule. She'll even do full training weekends if we want. Why?"

Just then a booming male voice called out from a nearby room.

"Is Magda still here, Meadow, or do we have guests?"

"Come in, babe," she called back. "We have representatives from the LAPD here. They have some questions about Taylor."

"Taylor who?" the man asked as he rounded the corner.

As he stood in the doorway, Jessie took him in. For a man in his mid-forties who likely worked many sixteen-hour days, he looked surprisingly spry. He was medium height, maybe five foot ten, with graying, light brown hair and thin-framed glasses. He wasn't as ripped as his wife, but he was trim and seemed to be in good shape. He looked at Jessie and Ryan expectantly.

"Taylor, our trainer," his wife reminded him, clearly irked but trying to hide it. "She was at the house just last weekend."

"I know who she is," he responded tartly. "It's just that I know more than one Taylor. I wasn't sure which one this was about."

"It's about Taylor Jansen," Ryan said, standing up to his full height as he shook the doctor's hand. "I'm Detective Hernandez and this Jessie Hunt. We were hoping your wife could answer a few questions about Ms. Jansen for us."

"We both can," Meadow Horsley replied. "Like I said, she trained us both. What is this about anyway? Is Taylor okay? I haven't heard from her in days."

"We were actually hoping to discuss this matter with you privately if we could, Mrs. Horsley," Ryan said. "It's of a somewhat sensitive nature."

"Don't be silly," she said, waving dismissively. "Anything you want to ask me, you can ask in front of my husband. I have no secrets."

"Are you sure?" Jessie asked, raising her eyebrows suggestively.

"I'm sure. Have at it."

Jessie and Ryan traded shrugs.

"Okay," he began. "In the course of an investigation we're pursuing, we came across several suggestive communications between you and Ms. Jansen."

Meadow Horsley nodded and replied matter-of-factly.

"You're talking about the sex tweets?"

CHAPTER TWELVE

Jessie's eyes went wide. Ryan tried to suppress a cough before replying.

"Yes. I'm talking about the sex tweets."

"It was a hell of a lot more than just tweets," she said, smiling broadly. "I'm assuming that if you saw the DMs, you also saw the photos. And if you saw the photos, you can probably guess what else was going on."

Ryan plowed ahead, trying to keep as straight a face as possible.

"So, you acknowledge that you were involved with Taylor physically, that you were carrying on an affair."

"I acknowledge the first part," Meadow said pointedly. "Not the second. We were sleeping together. But it wasn't an affair. Cal knew all about it. In fact, sometimes he watched."

Ryan and Jessie looked over at Cal, who nodded his confirmation.

"Just good, clean, adult fun," he said, as casual as his wife about the matter.

"Well, sometimes it was a little dirty," Meadow giggled.

"Can you elaborate?" Jessie asked, trying not to sound uncomfortable. If these folks were willing to be forthcoming, she and Ryan needed to take advantage of the chattiness, even if it caused some blushing. After all, they might not be so open later.

"Sure," Meadow said, sounding like she was about to discuss a PTA meeting. "We like to play games."

"What kind of games?" Jessie heard herself ask.

"You sure you can handle it, Ms. Hunt?" she asked. "You look like you got a sunburn in just the last five seconds."

Jessie ordered herself not to get any more flustered than she already was.

"Don't mind me. What kind of games?"

"Mostly light BDSM."

"What's that?" Ryan asked. Jessie was pretty sure he knew. But she was glad he was asking. It would allow her to gauge the Horsleys' physical responses as they answered.

"It stands for several things, including bondage and discipline, dominance and submission and sadomasochism," Cal explained with a dreamy smile. "For us, it included a lot of tying people up. We'd use padded cuffs, restraints, that kind of thing. We don't go in for whips or clamps. Very straightforward, all-American stuff."

"Sounds pretty tame," Jessie said, pleased that her tone couldn't be pegged as either sincere or sarcastic.

"It is," Meadow admitted, her eyes blazing in delight. "Sometimes we'd go a bit farther and add in a little auto-erotic asphyxiation. But we were very careful about that. We never did it without Cal there to observe and step in if need be. It's nice to have a physician in the family."

Ryan looked at Cal, in either genuine or feigned confusion. The doctor explained patiently.

"That means one of them would strangle the other—not to the point of putting her in danger—but enough to sometimes cause unconsciousness."

"Why?" Ryan asked.

Meadow took over the explanation.

"At that point just before you lose consciousness, you can get this amazing, sexual rush. It's an extra level of arousal on top of the standard one."

"But you have to be careful," Cal cautioned. "It's not something to just try on a lark."

"So you two make sure to ease in slowly," Meadow said, quivering with pleasure at her own quip.

Jessie refused to look at Ryan, who appeared unfazed.

"And you never participated?" he asked Cal.

"I like to watch," he said firmly.

Ryan turned his attention back to Meadow.

"When did you last... play games with Taylor?" he asked.

"She came over on Saturday," Meadow answered with a slight pout, apparently irked that she couldn't get a rise out of either of them. "I was hoping that we could get together with her this week, but she hasn't returned any of my texts. And she missed our training session this morning without cancelling. I was pissed but now I'm really starting to get worried. We've answered all your questions. Please tell us what's going on."

Jessie and Ryan traded looks. They couldn't hold off any longer. Besides, Jessie was anxious to watch the couple's reaction to the news. She nodded at Ryan to indicate that he should tell them while she watched. He began to speak.

"I have some bad news," he started. "Taylor Jansen is dead."

He let the statement linger in the air. Jessie watched as the Horsleys processed what he said. Meadow's sunny disposition crumbled almost immediately. Her eyes went wide and tears brimmed at their edges. Cal just looked stunned, as if he wasn't sure what he'd just heard.

"Are you certain?" he asked quietly.

"We are," Ryan replied.

Meadow began to cry, whimpering softly at first, before giving way to occasional hiccup-sobs.

"How did this happen?" she finally managed to croak.

"We're not entirely sure yet. But we're pursuing all options. That's why we're here. We're speaking with everyone she regularly interacted with and your phone communications put you in that group."

"Of course," Cal said, blinking repeatedly as if he was trying to prevent tears from appearing. "How can we help?"

"Thanks," Jessie said softly, wanting to appear sympathetic even if it wasn't entirely genuine. "We appreciate your assistance. We know it's hard to process something like this. Our first question would be about how long you all were involved with Taylor."

Cal furrowed his brow as he tried to recall.

"I want to say around six weeks," he answered.

"No, it was closer to two months," Meadow corrected, sniffling. "I still remember the first time we hooked up. Don't you remember, babe? We had her over and she seemed as stunned as these guys when we proposed a collective get-together?"

"It all runs together after a while," he admitted.

"It doesn't run together for me," she said sharply. "I still remember that first time like it was yesterday. She seemed so professional and no-nonsense. But once she let down her guard, Taylor was something else entirely."

"How so?" Jessie asked.

"She was just so much more open and curious and . . . eager."

"I see," Jessie said, at a bit of a loss as to how to proceed.

"Don't get me wrong," Meadow continued, grabbing a tissue and blowing her nose. "I'm not saying we were in love or anything like that. It was just a fling. But she was fun. She was my friend. And she was a good person."

"Why didn't she respond to your texts?" Ryan asked, not noting his suspicion that Taylor might have been dead by the time they were sent. "Did you all have some kind of falling out?"

"Not at all," Meadow told him. "Like I said, we were together over the weekend. That's why I was so surprised when she didn't get back to me or show up for training this morning. Wait, you don't think . . . was that because she had already died?"

"We don't have all the details yet," Jessie said, quickly moving on. "How did Taylor seem to you in recent days?"

"What do you mean?" Meadow asked, her eyes narrowing.

"Did she seem like her normal self or in any way different than usual?"

"Are you suggesting she did this to herself?" Cal asked, sounding offended.

"We have to pursue every possibility," Jessie said.

"I get that," Meadow jumped in. "And I'm not claiming that Taylor and I were best friends or that I knew the inner workings of her mind. But I find it very hard to believe that a woman like that would kill herself. She was just too . . . driven. She had things she wanted to accomplish."

"Look," Cal added. "I understand that maybe the person she presented to the world wasn't exactly the same as who she was inside. But we did get to know her pretty intimately. And I never saw anything that suggested depression or anything close to that."

"Thank you for that, Dr. Horsley," Ryan said.

"Cal, please."

"All right, Cal. Then I hope you can understand that as uncomfortable as this is, we need to ask where you both were in recent days."

"Of course," Meadow said, pulling out her phone. "Let me check our calendar."

As she did, Cal walked over and sat down next to her. Jessie couldn't help but notice that was the first time she'd seen them in such close physical proximity. Having the LAPD show up hadn't gotten them to close ranks. Nor had the news that a friend and lover had died. Even now, they weren't touching each other. He was merely looking over her shoulder as she looked at her phone.

"When are we talking about?" Meadow asked.

"How about from Monday morning up until now?" Ryan told her, sounding as unassuming as he could, considering he was basically asking for their alibis. It was clear to Jessie that he didn't want to reveal the estimated time of death.

"Monday morning we were actually at the gym. I was supposed to have a training session but she asked to push it so she could meet with a first-time client. I saw her as we were both leaving. That was actually the last time I remember communicating with her."

"How did she seem then?" Jessie asked.

"Normal. Maybe a little harried. But she always seemed a little harried."

"Did you see her too?" Ryan asked Cal.

"No. I was running a bit late in the locker room. I didn't catch up with Meadow until the parking lot."

"Okay," Ryan continued. "So where were you other than that?"

"We drove to work together," Meadow said, scrolling through her phone. "I was there all day, planning for a fundraiser we were having that night."

"And I had two surgeries that day. One minor one was in the morning. The other was more involved. It ran all afternoon and later than expected into the evening."

"That's right," Meadow recalled. "I remember, you missed all but the very tail end of the event. He showed up in his tux ten minutes before the thing ended."

"That was annoying," Cal agreed. "I ended up changing back into my civvies right away. I hate those penguin suits."

"Anyway, we drove home together again that night. The next morning, Cal had a meeting with a cardiology group in Santa Barbara so I came up too to try to secure a few donations. We were there until late evening. And today we both went to work early. I had a board meeting and Cal had an early surgery. Then we came back for the massages. I think that catches us up."

"Are there people who can vouch for your whereabouts?" Ryan asked.

"Certainly for all of Monday and today," Cal assured them, sounding less put out than Jessie would have expected. "It was just us on Tuesday for the drive north. But we were both on calls a lot. And I gather you can check our location data too?"

"We can," Ryan confirmed. "It may end up being a formality but why don't you both write down a list of folks who can confirm your location during those days and we'll follow up."

Both Horsleys nodded. Meadow grabbed a notepad, tore off two sheets, and handed Cal a pen.

"Do you mind if I borrow your restroom?" Jessie asked, glancing at Ryan, who imperceptibly returned the look.

"Of course not," Meadow said. "It's back down the hallway we came from. It's the last door on the right just before the staircase."

Jessie got up and excused herself. When she was out of sight, she walked as quickly as possible without making extra noise. She reached the bathroom and turned on the light. But rather than entering, she closed the door and turned her attention to the stairwell.

The Horsleys had been accommodating in their answers and their willing-ness to share their schedules. They didn't seem to be hiding much of anything. But Jessie knew it was unlikely that she'd get a chance like this again. So instead of just following standard procedure, she did something she knew would make Captain Decker pull out what little hair he had left.

She darted upstairs to invade their privacy.

CHAPTER THIRTEEN

Jessie knew she didn't have long.

Ryan had clearly understood what she was up to and would do his best to stall the Horsleys. But she had a finite amount of time to snoop before they would get suspicious and start wondering where she was.

The couple seemed credible. But in Jessie's experience, how people seemed and how they actually were could differ greatly. She preferred not to depend on their self-descriptions.

At the top of the stairs, she walked quickly down the hall, peeking into each room until she found what she could tell was the master bedroom. As she walked through to the bathroom, she glanced around. There were no leather bodysuits lying on the bed or handcuffs on the floor but she hadn't really expected to find that. She was more interested in what was in their medicine cabinet than their sex toy closet.

When she got in the bathroom, she found that each Horsley actually had their own cabinet. She opened the one closest to the door. She assumed it was Cal's because of the razor and shaving cream resting near the sink. It was filled with all kinds of over-the-counter medications but nothing in a prescription bottle and nothing that seemed out of the ordinary. She snapped a quick photo before moving on to Meadow's.

It had a few prescription bottles, only one of which she recognized as suspicious. It was an anti-anxiety medication she'd taken on a few occasions herself. It had an unfortunate side effect—it could cause sleepiness in some patients.

Jessie snapped a photo of that cabinet too, though she was disappointed by what she found. Nothing she saw here, not even Meadow's anti-anxiety med, seemed like an obvious candidate for drugging Taylor.

She was just closing the cabinet when she got a text from Ryan with one word: "restless." Quickly, she darted out of the room, tiptoed back down the hall and traversed the stairs as quietly as possible. She was just about to round the corner to get back to the hallway with the bathroom when she heard Meadow's voice.

"...just make sure she's okay. I can offer her something if she's struggling."

The voice was accompanied by the sounds of her approaching footsteps. There was no way for Jessie to access the bathroom without being seen. Then she heard another voice—Ryan's.

"Can I give you something for her, Mrs. Horsley?" he called out from the far end of the hall. "Jessie was complaining of stomach discomfort on the way over here and I have a tablet that might help with that."

"Sure, and call me Meadow," Meadow insisted, her voice now sounding slightly more distant.

Jessie peeked around the corner and saw her walking back toward Ryan, who was rifling through his pockets as he stared desperately down the hall. As unobtrusively as possible, she darted around the corner, catching the detective's eye as she opened the bathroom door, stepped inside and closed it again after her. She pressed her ear against the door and could hear what she thought was Ryan saying he must have made a mistake and that he didn't actually have anything.

Deciding not to test her luck any farther, she moved over to the toilet and flushed it. After leisurely washing her hands, she opened the door and stepped back into the hall. She was alone. Meadow must have heard the flush and decided it would be rude to loiter outside the bathroom door. Jessie walked back down the hall to the living room, trying not to look like someone with something to hide.

The three of them were sitting on the couches, clearly hoping not to appear like they were waiting for her return, though they obviously were.

"Sorry I took so long," Jessie said, sounding as sheepish as she could. "Last time I'll go to Pink's for lunch on a workday."

"No problem," Meadow said, looking genuinely concerned. "Can we get you anything?"

"No, I'm okay now. Sorry for the hassle."

Ryan stood up and took the initiative to end the interview.

"We've got the contact info for everyone so I think that's all we need for now," he said authoritatively. "I assume you won't mind if we need to return to ask a few more questions at some point."

"Whatever we can do to help," Meadow said, taking Cal's hand for the first time. He seemed surprised by the action.

"Yes," he agreed. "If there's anything more we can do, just let us know."

"We'll be in touch," Jessie promised as they headed for the main entrance. "No need to walk us out."

As they walked down the long hallway back to the front door, Ryan leaned over and muttered to her.

"Cut that kind of close, don't you think?"

"I just wanted to give you a chance to work on your improvisational acting skills," she teased.

"If solving this case depends on my acting skills, we're in real trouble."

"I tend to agree," she said.

She didn't look over at him but she knew he was smiling.

"So you're saying you almost got caught doing an illegal search of their bathroom for nothing?" Ryan asked as they drove from the Horsley home back to the station.

"I wouldn't say *nothing*," Jessie countered. "At least now we know that they have something that could have been used to drug Taylor."

"But you said that it works as a mild sedative in some patients. That doesn't seem like the ideal delivery system to drug someone to death. Besides, I would think a doctor could secure a more efficient drug to get the job done. This seems like a stretch to me. I'm still leaning toward the suicide angle."

"Even though not a single person we've spoke to said they could envision her killing herself?" Jessie asked incredulously.

"Like you said, you didn't know your husband was a sociopath and you'd been with him for years."

"Yes," Jessie agreed, though she didn't love having her personal history used against her in a discussion of a case. "But he was actively trying to hide that from me. It was like a second job for him. It's hard to imagine Taylor being able to maintain that kind of façade as effectively. I just think we need to double check these Horsley alibis. Like you said before, people this good aren't to be trusted."

"I stand by that. But at least initially, their alibis seem pretty ironclad."

Jessie couldn't disagree.

"Let's give these phone numbers to the guys back at the office," she suggested. "Maybe they can follow up with some of the alibi witnesses."

"What guys back at the office?" Ryan reminded her. "They're all still on the gang case. We're on our own with this one."

"Okay. Then we can at least have tech trace their car and phone signals to confirm everything they said about being at the hospital on Monday and in Santa Barbara on Tuesday. And we may as well call the medical examiner's office now to see what Lorne thinks about whether Xanax could be used as a sedative."

They did just that. When Lorne answered, he sounded surprised to hear from them.

"That's weird," he said. "I was just about to call you."

"What's up?" Ryan asked.

"We found out more definitively what was in her system. It *was* a sedative."

"Xanax?" Jessie volunteered.

"No, why?"

"No reason," she said, deciding not to get into details. "There's no way it could have been that though?"

"No," Lorne assured her. "The quantity she would have had to consume for it to operate as a sedative strong enough to kill her would have shown up clearly. This was almost certainly a traditional sleeping pill like Eszopiclone. The dosage was more than is typically taken to get to sleep, probably the equivalent of five or six pills. That's most often seen in someone who takes a few, then forgets they did and takes a few more."

"That amount could kill someone?" Ryan asked, surprised.

"Almost certainly not. You'd require many more than that. But if the person rarely took them, it could have an outsized effect, really slow their respiration. I think that's what happened here. And it's why it took us so long to pin down a time of death. Her body was already operating at reduced function when she died."

"So you have a time of death?" Jessie asked.

"We have a window but it's still pretty rough. We think she died between noon on Monday and 4 a.m. on Tuesday morning."

"That helps some," Ryan said.

"But I'm still confused," Jessie added. "If the pills didn't kill her, what did?"

"Hard to be sure," Lorne replied. "There are some signs that she may have suffocated. She could have rolled over and choked on a pillow. If she was that incapacitated by the medication, she might not have been able to reflexively pull herself away from something blocking her airway. Or, if she had another condition, like asthma, and had an attack while sedated, that could present as suffocation too."

"So you're saying it's unlikely that she took enough pills to consider this a suicide?" Jessie reiterated.

"It would be unusual for someone attempting to take her own life to take so few," Lorne conceded.

"But you're also saying that it doesn't seem like she was drugged," Ryan added. "Or that anyone actively took measures to stop her breathing. This might just be an unfortunate accident?"

"It's possible." Lorne allowed.

"Okay, thanks, Lorne," Ryan replied. "We'll get back to you if we have other questions."

After they hung up, he looked over at Jessie.

"Is it possible that we're investigating this thing as a potential homicide and it's just a series of horrible coincidences?"

"I wouldn't rule anything out at this point," Jessie said, frustrated. "I'm more inclined to accept the 'accidental death' theory than the suicide one. But I don't feel great about that either."

"Why?" Ryan asked.

"There are just a lot of things that don't add up to me. We have Lorne's window for time of death. But based on her lack of communication after Monday morning, I'm going to assume that she ingested that medication before noon that day. Why didn't we find any other sleeping pills at her place? And she's a hardcore health and fitness professional—why would she take any sleeping pills, especially in the middle of the day? We've seen nothing that would suggest she felt she needed to."

"She was pregnant too, which you'd think would make her cautious with meds," Ryan reminded her.

"Right, she seems like the type to keep her system as clean as possible. But we don't know if she even knew that she was pregnant. And if she did, why would she have taken multiple sleeping pills?"

"Maybe to induce a miscarriage?" Ryan suggested.

"By taking five or six pills?" Jessie asked skeptically. "That seems unlikely. Plus there was the open window. That's a lot going on at once."

Ryan started to respond when his phone rang.

"It's Officer Dooley," he said.

"Put him on speaker," Jessie replied.

"Hey Dooley," Ryan said after hitting the button. "You didn't shoot anyone since we last saw you, did you?"

"No, Detective," Dooley said, sounding hangdog even over the phone. "I just wanted to let you know that Gavin Peck just pulled up in front of his house. He's going inside."

"How does he look? Guilty?"

"He looks sweaty, sir. I think he just came from the gym. He's in shorts and a very tight tank top."

"Good job, Dooley," Ryan said. "That's an extremely vivid description. Why don't you and your partner hang out there. We're not too far away. We can be there in twenty minutes. Maybe he'll have showered by the time we arrive. Let us know if anything changes in the interim."

"Yes, sir."

"And Dooley," Ryan added, an impish smile on his face. "Try not to shoot him while you wait."

He hung up before Dooley could respond.

"You," Jessie said, trying not to laugh, "are a first-rate jerk."

CHAPTER FOURTEEN

Jessie sensed trouble.

Even before they knocked on Peck's door, one look at his vehicle gave her the sense that this was a guy with a chip on his shoulder. He drove an oversized black pickup truck that took up most of his small driveway. It was immaculate, shiny and dust-free, as if it had been waxed before he drove it over.

While it was unwise to draw too many conclusions from what kind of car a person drove, it was hard for Jessie *not* to make assumptions about a muscle-bound single guy in a big city who drove a huge, spotless truck that looked to have never hauled anything. Appearing strong was obviously a priority for Gavin Peck.

She and Ryan briefly checked in with Dooley and his partner, a large, quiet guy named Beecher, before heading over. They decided they might have more luck with a casual approach, rather than knocking on his door with two uniformed officers beside them, so they left them down the street and out of sight in the black and white.

"How do you think we should play this?" Ryan said as they approached the front door.

"Authoritative but not intimidating, I think," Jessie suggested. "We want him to know who's in charge but not get overly defensive."

"Sounds reasonable," Ryan agreed. "Let's just hope he hasn't just injected his steroids for the day."

Jessie smiled appreciatively as she knocked on the door. They only had to wait a few seconds for a response.

"Who is it?" a thundering voice demanded from behind the heavy wooden door.

"My name is Jessie Hunt, Gavin," she said, intentionally using his first name to break down the formality of the situation. "I'm here with Ryan Hernandez.

We work with local law enforcement. We were hoping to ask you a few questions about an acquaintance of yours."

Within moments, the door opened so that the only separation between them was the screen door. Jessie, who had only seen close-up photos of Gavin Peck, took him in. He was quite a sight to behold.

Gavin Peck was about her height, maybe five foot ten. But he was easily 230 pounds and every inch of it appeared to be muscle. He was wearing blue jeans and a plain white T-shirt, both of which looked to be intentionally several sizes too small for him. His thick neck connected to a too-tanned face with shockingly blue eyes and jet-black hair that was still wet from his shower. His biceps bulged and long ropy veins ran down his arms before spidering out along his broad forearms. It was both impressive and a little gross.

"Is this about the guy down the street?" he asked, sounding annoyed. "I already agreed not to blast my music when I'm driving by. I told that cop I'd wait until I was out of the neighborhood. This doesn't seem like the kind of thing that requires a second visit from the LAPD."

"It's not," Ryan confirmed. "That's not why we're here."

"What then?"

"It's about Taylor," Jessie said.

The confused look on Gavin's face turned immediately into aggravation.

"What now?" he pressed. "Don't tell me she filed a restraining order. I've barely talked to her in the last few weeks."

"That's not entirely true, Gavin," Ryan said in a leading but not-quite-accusatory tone. "You called her just last week."

Gavin paused for a moment, now getting that the people in front of him couldn't be so easily snowed.

"Yeah, but it wasn't any big deal. I just asked if she was happy. I thought she might be open to getting back together."

"And was she?" Jessie wondered.

Gavin looked at her quizzically.

"What did she say?" he asked.

The truth was, Jessie had no idea. While Taylor's phone records showed a call from Gavin last Thursday evening that lasted about four minutes, they had no way of knowing the content. He could be telling the truth. One would have thought that if the call was confrontational or threatening, she would have hung up well before the four-minute mark. Or maybe she was trying to talk him down. Jessie hoped that he might let her know accidentally.

"I think you can guess how she would describe it," she said, hoping her vagueness would prompt a defensive response.

"No, I really don't," he said, not taking the bait. "Other than that, nothing I said would make her sic the cops on me. So there must be something else going on. Who exactly are you two with again?"

"LAPD," Ryan said. "I'm a detective and Jessie here consults."

Jessie admired the attempt. It was clear that Ryan was hoping that by neglecting to mention that he was a homicide detective and that Jessie was a criminal profiler, they could keep Gavin from jumping to conclusions. But it didn't work.

"That's a pretty imprecise description," Gavin said, calling him on it. "Look, here's what I know. I don't think you have any idea what Jessie and I discussed. I think you're fishing. I also think that if she had filed a restraining order against me, it would just be delivered. I wouldn't be questioned on my doorstep by a detective and a 'consultant' who are clearly trying to keep things from me. I also doubt you'd have those officers sitting in the police car down the street. Something else is going on here. So you can either tell me or you can leave."

Jessie glanced over at Ryan, who seemed uncertain whether to come clean or not. She didn't think they had much choice. Gavin was closing down. If she was going to gauge his genuine reaction when they told him why they were there, they needed to do it now. She could already see in his eyes that he was starting to figure things out.

"Taylor's dead, Gavin," she said flatly.

CHAPTER FIFTEEN

"Wait, what?" he asked.

He still had the defiant look on his face, as if he hadn't fully processed her words and was having the previous conversation.

"Taylor Jansen is dead," she repeated, neither sympathetically nor accusatorily. "Her body was found this morning. So we are talking to everyone she knew. She knew you."

He opened his mouth but no words came out. Then he closed it again. He looked at the floor and then back at the two of them as if they might tell him at any moment that they were only joking.

"Do you want to sit down?" she asked, pointing at the living room couch behind him.

He nodded, walked over and took a seat. He was looking in their general direction but Jessie saw that he wasn't really looking at them at all. His thoughts were elsewhere.

As Jessie waited for him, she glanced around the house, trying not to appear obvious. He had even more tubs of protein powder than Taylor, along with countless boxes of bars and electrolyte drinks, all stacked neatly against one wall. Down the hall, she could see a bedroom that had been converted into a home gym, with a bench and a rack of free weights.

The house was far more lived in than Taylor's place. There were prints on the wall and posters from obscure music festivals. His furniture looked like he had actually put thought into it. And he even had a couple of plants. His house looked like Jessie imagined Taylor's would and vice versa.

"Are you sure?" Gavin asked, pulling her back into the moment. "Where was she found?"

"I'm afraid we can't get into the details, Gavin," she said. "But we are sure. We were hoping you could help us out."

"How?"

"By telling us where you were on Monday afternoon and evening," Ryan said a little more forcefully than Jessie thought was necessary. Gavin clearly agreed because when he turned to look at the detective, his eyes were blazing.

"Why are you asking me that? Was she killed? Are you suggesting I killed her?"

Jessie tried to lower the temperature.

"We're not suggesting anything, Gavin. We're investigators. We're gathering information. You aren't the first or the only person we've spoken to today. And you won't be the last. We have to cover all our bases. So we'd really appreciate you giving us a timeline of where you were on Monday."

"I loved her, you know. I would never hurt her. Even after she broke it off, when I was at my most upset, I would never have done anything…"

His words were interrupted by choked sob. He took a moment to regroup and finished his thought.

"I always thought we'd eventually reconnect, you know?"

"Of course," Jessie said. "We always think we have more time. Unfortunately, it doesn't always work out that way. That's where we come in, Gavin. It's our job to determine what happened and if necessary, get justice for it. You can help us with that. The sooner we can move on to other leads, the more likely we are to figure out what happened to Taylor. Can you help us with that, please?"

He looked at her absently. After a few seconds, he nodded.

"What day again?" he asked quietly.

"Monday," Jessie reminded him.

"Monday," he said, reaching into his pocket, making Ryan stiffen imperceptibly before he realized Gavin Peck was going for his phone to check his calendar. "I was here most of the day, working."

"What do you do?" Jessie asked.

"I'm a freelance web designer. I work from home for most of my jobs."

"We'll need the name of the client you were working for that day," Ryan said.

Gavin's head snapped in his direction. All the anger Jessie had managed to defuse was percolating again. Jessie said nothing, hoping things would settle on their own.

Ryan Hernandez was much more experienced than she was. But for whatever reason, whether it was being out of practice, recovering from injury or being mid-divorce, he seemed off his game. The pre-stabbing Detective Hernandez wouldn't poke the bear like this.

"Hey man," Gavin said irritably. "I know you need my frickin' alibi. I'm trying to give it you. You don't have to be a total asshole about it."

"You realize you are talking to an LAPD detective, right?" Ryan asked, not making much effort to cool things off.

"I realize that just because you're a cop doesn't mean you can treat me like crap. I realize I could tell you to leave and lawyer up just to make things hard for you."

"That would make you look awful suspicious, Gavin," Ryan shot back.

"You already obviously think I'm guilty, man!" Gavin said, suddenly standing up.

Jessie groaned to herself.

Oh Gavin, that was a mistake.

Ryan, who was already standing squared up at the shorter but thicker man.

"I know it's hard to contain yourself with all the 'roids coursing through your system. But maybe you should sit back down, Mr. Peck," he said forcefully.

"Now you're accusing me of juicing too? Maybe I should kick your scrawny ass," Gavin retorted.

"I know you're not threatening a member of law enforcement, Mr. Peck," Ryan said quietly, "because that would be grounds for arrest. Do you want to get arrested, Mr. Peck?"

"I want you to stop hassling me, man," Gavin retorted, taking another step forward.

"Gavin, please settle down," Jessie pleaded, though she was looking at Ryan and trying to convey the same thing to him with her eyes

But Ryan wasn't looking at her.

"Yeah, settle down, Gavin," he said, staring at the increasingly agitated man in front of him. "It doesn't take much to set you off, does it? Is this how you acted around Taylor? You look like you're about to pop a vessel."

"I'm gonna pop you," Gavin said, suddenly taking a swing.

It was wide and sloppy and Ryan was able to deflect it and react with a gut punch of his own. Gavin doubled over as Ryan took a stumble backward and inhaled deeply. He winced as if the effort of throwing the punch had tweaked something. Jessie was about to ask him if he was okay when Gavin, still bent over, unexpectedly dove at Ryan.

He smashed into the detective and they collapsed together on the floor. On top, Gavin began to throw punches at the detective underneath him. Jessie briefly considered trying to knock him off the smaller man but thought better of it. Instead she pulled a Taser out of a holster on her belt and jammed it against Gavin's neck.

The man convulsed for a few seconds before loosening his grip on Ryan. Jessie used the moment to kick him off the detective. He toppled over, though he looked like he was regrouping to get up again. Jessie, realizing she wouldn't have the element of surprise on her side anymore if he did, hurried to the screen door and called down the street.

"Dooley, Beecher—we've got a rowdy suspect. We need your help now!"

When she saw the two of them running her way, she turned back to the men lying on the floor. Ryan was flat on his back, clutching his side and gasping for breath. Gavin Peck, who looked disoriented, was trying to get from his stomach to his knees.

"Stay down, Gavin," she ordered as authoritatively as she could. "This is bad for you. But it could get a lot worse. I don't want to have to shoot you."

She wasn't sure if he couldn't hear her or was simply ignoring her. Either way, Gavin was now on his hands and knees and seemed to be gathering himself to jump at Ryan again. Jessie holstered her Taser and grabbed Ryan's free hand, dragging him along the floor and out of leaping range.

Gavin looked up at her with watery eyes and moved his mouth, trying to form words she couldn't decipher. She undid her gun holster and rested her hand there.

"I don't understand what you're saying, Gavin. But you need to stay put until we can work this out. Please don't make any sudden movements. No amount of bench pressing is going to protect you from a bullet."

Just then, Dooley and Beecher burst through the door. They took one look at the situation and both reached for their guns.

"No! Not necessary!" Jessie yelled. "Just take him into custody."

Dooley looked at her hesitantly and only did as she said when she raised her eyebrows in her best "are you questioning me" way. That was enough to chasten him. He moved quickly to cuff Gavin as Beecher stood over his shoulder. Jessie looked down at Ryan, who seemed to be trying not to groan.

"I swear," she muttered at him, "if that guy hadn't already kicked your ass, I'd do it myself."

Chapter Sixteen

The sirens blared.

Jessie watched the ambulance go, knowing that she was sure to get grief for having called it in the first place. But she hadn't had a choice at the time.

As Beecher escorted Gavin Peck to the police car to be taken to the station, Dooley took one look at Ryan, desperately trying to mask his discomfort, and shook his head.

"Either you can call for the EMTs or I will," he said to her. "That guy is doing his best to hide it but he is in serious pain. I know he was a jerk to me but I feel bad for him anyway."

"I'll drive him in to get checked out," Jessie had assured him.

"No way. I don't trust that he'll actually end up being seen unless the EMTs do it officially. I'm not getting my service record docked because your partner is a stubborn sonofabitch."

In the end Jessie made the call for medical assistance because she figured Ryan wouldn't come down on her as hard as Dooley. It was a sign of just how much distress he was in that he only cursed briefly at her before being carted off on the gurney.

"I'm fine," he'd insisted through gritted teeth.

"Great. Glad to hear it," she replied. "Then you'll be super fine when I pick you up after the doctors have given you the all clear."

He was still muttering at her when they'd slammed the back of the ambulance doors shut. When he was gone, she decided to head back to the station to interview Gavin while he was still raw. She figured she was more likely to get something useful out of him when he felt vulnerable.

On the way over, she called Kat to see if she'd made any progress in her investigation on Hannah's background. Her friend picked up on the second ring.

"Are you kidding me?" she asked when she realized what Jessie was after. "It's only been a few hours. Can you at least give me until the end of the workday before you start pestering me, you control freak?"

"Sorry," Jessie said as she drove along the clogged late-afternoon streets. "I guess I'm just trying to keep busy here. Ryan got himself re-injured playing tough guy with a short-tempered weightlifter, who I now get to interrogate."

Kat groaned.

"That guy is almost as bad as you when it comes to self-destructive decision-making."

"Hey," Jessie protested. "I hold the championship belt on that one and it's not even close."

"I stand corrected," Kat said. "Why don't you check in with me after your interrogation of this guy? Maybe I'll have something for you by then."

Jessie agreed and hung up. She was tempted to go by Hannah's house again but told her herself that not only was the timing crucial for this Peck interview, it was just generally a terrible idea. By the time she'd finally convinced herself, it was moot. She had passed the turnoff for the neighborhood.

It turned out to be a good decision. When she arrived at the station, she was able to use the questioning as an excuse not to check in with Decker. Instead she headed straight to the interrogation room and looked through the one-way glass.

Gavin Peck was sitting in a chair bolted to the floor, his hand cuffed to a table that was also secured. He looked to be both agitated and remorseful, an excellent combination for an interrogation. She walked in.

"You cooled off a bit, Gavin?" she asked, doing her best to keep any judgment out of her voice.

"Has your partner?" he shot back.

"He's still working through it," she said, deciding not to mention the hospital trip. She didn't need to add any additional pressure to the conversation. "That's why it'll just be me for now. I was hoping we could continue our chat about where you were on Monday."

"I was going to tell you before that detective got all Dirty Harry on me," he pouted.

"Well, you can tell me now."

Gavin looked at her, seemingly debating whether he should. In the end, he seemed to decide that obstinacy wasn't doing him any good.

"I *was* going to say that I was working from home most of Monday, then was at the gym in the late afternoon and evening," he answered.

"I assume we'll be able to confirm that with your client and by checking activity on your computer and phone?"

"I assume so too," he replied snarkily.

"Maybe not the best way to go with this," Jessie reminded him. "For the record, we have a police report of a dispute between you and your ex-girlfriend, who is now dead. And when asked about your alibi during her time of death, you assaulted a police officer. Those facts are troubling, regardless of the context, Gavin."

The clarity of that summation seemed to hit him hard. His scowl faded, replaced by a distraught expression.

"Do you need to read me my rights?" he finally asked.

She wasn't a cop so she wasn't sure herself but decided to bluster her way through it.

"I don't know. Do I? I thought we were just talking. But if it'll make you feel better we can."

She called in the officer standing guard outside the room, an enthusiastic rookie named Beatty. As if she was doing Gavin a favor, she had him recite the Miranda warning. When Beatty left the room, she looked at the suspect expectantly. It didn't take long.

"Listen," he implored, "I know it looks bad. But I didn't do this. I loved Taylor. I wanted her back. But I knew she'd never return for good. I just wasn't enough for her."

"What does that mean?" Jessie asked, her fingertips tingling slightly.

"She just..." he started, apparently unsure whether he should reveal what he was about to say. "She just wanted more than I could give her."

"What did she want, Gavin?"

"Look, you have to understand, Taylor was relentless in how she lived. Most trainers at that gym have five to seven clients each day. She had eight to ten. She rarely slept but she never seemed tired. She got bored real easily and just seemed to need constant stimulation. This isn't just sour grapes. I don't think any traditional relationship would have satisfied her. In fact, I know it."

Jessie was growing frustrated with his cryptic comments. She couldn't decide whether they were intentionally vague or if he was just reluctant to speak ill of the dead.

"Gavin, I'm going to be straight with you—you need to be more direct with me," she insisted. "We'll check out your alibi. But right now, you are a person of interest in Taylor's death. So whatever it is you're carefully not telling me, now's the time to spit it out. You're not helping yourself by playing coy."

"Okay, but nothing I say can be used against me, right?"

"Wrong," she said incredulously. "Everything you say can be used against you. But…if you didn't kill Taylor, it probably won't be. Still, it's your call. If you're innocent, I'd assume you'd do everything you could to help us find out what happened."

"All right. I never stalked her but sometimes I did follow her from work to see where she was going."

Jessie fought the strong urge to point out that what he was describing was the very definition of stalking.

"Go on," she muttered instead.

"So, this one time, about a week after she broke up with me, I followed her to this house in the hills. She parked on the street and walked up to this fancy house. I sat out front for a while, debating what to do. Finally, I walked up the driveway and peeked through a few windows. That's when I saw her."

He paused. Jessie thought it was for dramatic effect but realized he had stopped entirely. It was like he had changed his mind mid-story.

"What was she doing, Gavin?" she pressed.

After about five seconds that felt like an eternity, he spoke.

"She was in this candlelit dining room. She was there with a man and…another woman. All three of them were naked. She and the man were doing things to each other that I'd rather not describe. The man was wearing a mask. And the woman was pouring drops of hot candle wax on them."

While this wasn't exactly what the Horsleys had described, it was in the same universe. However, Meadow had insisted that Cal only watched. It sounded like that hadn't been totally accurate.

"This house was off Griffith Park Boulevard?" she confirmed.

"What? No. It was on Outpost Circle just north of Franklin, near the Magic Castle."

"Are you sure?" Jessie asked.

"Of course. It's only blocks north of my place. Every time I pass the cross street I have to block the image out of my head."

"What did the couple look like?" Jessie demanded. Her perfectly ordered personality profile of Taylor Jansen was crumbling before her.

"The woman was skinny and blond—maybe thirty-five. The guy was about the same age. I tried not to look at him much but he was tall and built for a thin guy. He had longish black hair, kind of wavy. I couldn't describe his face."

"He didn't wear glasses?" she asked.

"Like I said, he wore a mask. Why?"

"Just checking. Did you get their names?" Jessie wanted to know. She could tell her unsettled demeanor was making him nervous, so she did her best to rein it in.

"Not then but, well, I looked up the address later and got them," he admitted sheepishly.

"What were their names, Gavin?"

"Doug and Claire Shine," he said. "It turns out she was a client of Taylor's."

"How do you know that?"

"She told me. That's what our argument was about that night in the parking garage. I confronted her with what I'd seen. She got pissed at me for snooping. I told her she wasn't the person I thought she was. And she said I was right. That's when the cop showed up. And that's why she didn't push for any kind of restraining order. She would have had to explain why she wanted it. And then what she'd done would have come out. She didn't want that."

Jessie's mind was reeling. In addition to the Horsleys, Taylor was sexually involved with an entirely different couple. How many of them were there?

Gavin was looking at her like he expected more questions so she asked one.

"Did she tell you anything else when you confronted her about this couple? Did she say how long it had been going on with them?"

"Not long. She said she did it on a lark right after our breakup. She said she'd decided she needed to live the life she wanted and not the one that was expected of her. She wanted to explore different sides of herself. So I have that to hold on to."

"What's 'that'?" Jessie asked.

"That I was catalyst for her pursuing S&M threesomes. It's a real ego boost."

Jessie looked at him, not sure whether to offer condolences or laugh. She managed to avoid either, standing up and nodding.

"Thanks for your help, Gavin. I'm afraid you're stuck here overnight at least. But if your alibi holds up and your info proves useful, I might try to convince Detective Hernandez to drop the charges against you. So be on your best behavior, okay?"

"Okay," he replied pathetically.

She stepped out and walked down the hall, barely aware of the people around her. Her mind was racing. How had Taylor kept a lid on this part of her life? Was it really something she'd only started pursuing in recent months or was that just a story for Gavin? And most important, did these new lifestyle choices have anything to do with her death or was it just a coincidence? There was still no definitive proof that she'd been murdered. Whether Jessie bought them or not, she had to admit that there were still reasonable arguments to be made for both suicide and accidental death.

She also couldn't help but wonder what the deal was with Gavin. When she'd first seen him, she assumed he was some meathead who spent all his time at the gym. And there was definitely that aspect to him. But he was no dummy. He did well enough as a web designer to own his own home in the Hollywood Hills by thirty-two.

She couldn't dismiss the possibility that this whole "spurned boyfriend pining for his girl and wrecked by her death" image was a sham. It was possible that he was just a mopey guy who peeped on his ex out of longing. Or he could be admitting to that to distract from the possibility that he was far more than just a peeping Tom.

She was turning the options over in her head when she was shaken from her reverie by the sight of Captain Decker at the far end of the hall. He hadn't seen her yet. But she knew the minute he did, she'd be called into his office to explain what happened with Ryan. They'd almost certainly be taken off the case. She looked around desperately. There was nowhere to hide.

CHAPTER SEVENTEEN

She was tempted to crawl.

If it kept her out of the Captain's sightline it would be worth it. Luckily she didn't have to.

As she turned around, she inadvertently bumped into a burly officer headed in the same direction that she wanted to go. The collision didn't hurt her but she used it as an excuse to grab him and pull him toward her.

"Sorry, Officer," she apologized, making sure that she positioned the man between her and Decker. "I thought I might take a tumble there for a second. Are you okay?"

"I'm fine, ma'am. Are you?"

"Yes, thanks. I'm good—just in a hurry as always."

Without another word, she quickly darted back down the hall away from Decker, making sure to walk in front of the large cop until she could dash into the ladies' room.

She waited a good two minutes before poking her head out. Seeing that the coast was clear, she dashed back down the hall to the parking garage. She didn't want to risk calling to check on Ryan from her desk.

Sitting in the relative comfort of the car, she called the hospital and got word that he was under precautionary observation and she could pick him up in about an hour. She checked the time. It was 5:45. She saw that while she was on the phone, Kat had texted her. It read:

"Info for you. Meet for download and drinks at 6 p.m. You know where."

Jessie did know. It was the same watering hole, actually called the Watering Hole, that they'd been meeting at regularly ever since both felt safe going out in public again. It was nice not being hunted by serial killers. She decided she could pop over briefly and texted Kat that she would meet her in fifteen minutes.

When she arrived, Kat was already at the bar, saving a stool for her. Her friend waved her over with a smile on her face. As she maneuvered through the crowd comprised mostly of thirty-something financial types looking to take advantage of happy hour, Jessie noted how much Kat's recent lifestyle change agreed with her.

Before, when she headed security at a lockdown facility for mentally unfit criminal offenders, mostly murderers and rapists, she walked around with a permanent frown. Her hair was always pulled back in a tight ponytail or bun and she wore a bland, unflattering security uniform. Now a private investigator answering to no one, she could wear civilian clothes, let her hair down and even wear makeup.

She was doing all of that now. As she stood up to meet Jessie, her loose, shoulder-length brown hair bounced. She wore slacks and a blouse that actually highlighted her well-built five-foot-seven, 140-pound body. Even with the long scar running down her left cheek from her eye to her mouth, she had a magnetism to her. Jessie, who towered over her, leaned down and the two women hugged.

"I ordered you a seven and seven," Kat said. "It sounded like you could use it."

"Thanks," Jessie replied. "But I can't stay too long. I have to pick up Ryan from the hospital in a bit."

"How's he doing?"

"I don't know for sure. But I'm assuming that since they're releasing him, it's nothing too bad. He's just pushing himself too hard, trying to look competent to the boss after being out of commission for a while."

"Are you sure he's not doing that because he wants to impress you?" Kat asked, a suggestive inflection in her voice.

"Are you back on that again?" Jessie moaned. For weeks now, her friend had been pressing her to make some kind of move to let Detective Hernandez know she was open to changing their personal dynamic. If Jessie told her about Ryan's admission this morning, it would only add fuel to an already raging fire, so she deflected. "Who would have thought a decorated Army Ranger would be such a gossip."

They both laughed as their drinks arrived. After the server left, Kat turned serious.

"I just want you to be happy, Jessie," she said earnestly. "This is the first time since I've known you that you're really free and clear. Your crazy ex-husband is in prison. Your psycho father is dead. Your not-so-secret serial killer admirer helped you defeat your psycho father and subsequently decided to leave you alone. Don't you think you've earned a bit of joy in your life?"

Jessie couldn't agree more but wasn't in the mood for a "seize the day" talk right now; maybe when she had more than half an hour.

"I will note your comments for the record. In the meantime, you said you have some info for me on Hannah."

"I do. But before I give it to you, let me ask you something. Have you considered *why* you are so fixated on this girl? I know you're related. But almost no one else knows about that connection. Your dad is dead. Bolton Crutchfield is gone. You are free to lead your life and let Hannah live hers. It's like you *want* to be tethered to the past."

Jessie sighed. There was merit to what Kat said. But there was also something else.

"She's my sister. I can't just ignore that, Kat."

"I get it," Kat said. "And I will tell you what you want to know. But you should also know this conversation isn't over. I'm not letting you off the hook. This is just a temporary reprieve."

"I know," Jessie assured her. "Now, I believe you are in my employ at the moment. So tell me what you found."

Kat shook her head in mock disgust. But she'd known Jessie long enough to realize pushing more wouldn't help. So she switched topics.

"Okay, I'm still doing some following up. It's a bit challenging since Hannah's a minor. But here's what I know for sure. It's unclear how your father met Hannah's mother, who was named Corinne Weatherly. She used to live in Chicago but moved out here to become an actress in her late teens.

"She was living in Santa Clarita when she got pregnant. No one I spoke to from back then recalls her having a steady boyfriend, though one neighbor in her apartment complex said she sometimes talked about an older guy she'd hook up with when he was in town for business."

"You think Xander was the older businessman?" Jessie asked.

"No way to know for sure. But the age and timeline fit. Plus we know your father was bouncing around the country at that time. Pretending to be a straight-arrow businessman who wore suits and ties would be a great cover for a serial killer from the Ozark backwoods."

"He wasn't originally from the back woods," Jessie noted unemotionally. "He just killed people there."

It was only when Kat's mouth dropped open in shock that Jessie realized the comment was perhaps a little blasé considering the subject matter.

"Sorry," she said. "Sometimes my appropriateness meter malfunctions. Please continue."

"Anyway," Kat said, trying to regroup. "At some point Corinne got into drugs. DCFS even briefly put Hannah into foster care. But that seemed to light a fire under Corinne, who went to rehab and got clean. She'd been one year sober when she was found dead in their apartment. Hannah was three."

"Did she fall off the wagon?" Jessie asked.

"Overdose was the official determination. But there were some lingering questions."

"Like?" Jessie pressed.

"Like, she died of a massive overdose. There was enough heroin in her system to kill three people. Apparently it was weird because the people she spoke to that afternoon said she seemed fine—no indication that anything was wrong or that she was having trouble."

"Still," Jessie pushed back, trying to keep an open mind, "sometimes when this kind of thing comes back, it comes back hard."

"That's true. But there were a few other things. Her windows and door were unlocked, which neighbors said was unusual. There were needles in both her arms, which makes absolutely no sense. And also, she had supposedly never taken heroin before. Opioids were her thing. And yet the official story is that, after working hard to get her daughter back and seeming to be doing well, she shot up a massive amount of a drug she had never used in both her arms at the same time. Not fishy at all."

Jessie couldn't disagree. Besides, this wouldn't be out of character for Xander Thurman. After all, he'd killed her own mother when she discovered he was a killer and tried to take her and escape from him. If he did something similar to Hannah's mom, it would fit his pattern of punishing women who wouldn't bend to his sick will.

"Was there an investigation?" she asked.

"Cursory," Kat said. "That's where I got some of this info. I also talked to one of the detectives assigned to the case. He's retired now and couldn't remember it until I refreshed him on his original case notes. It was fourteen years ago. After some prodding, he admitted that they didn't pursue many leads. There were no unusual fingerprints in the home, no sign of forced entry and no record of any conflicts with neighbors, acquaintances or lovers. And she was a known user. It was easy to mark it down as an OD and move on. So that's what they did."

She took a big gulp of air and an even longer gulp of her mojito. Jessie tried to play out her scenario.

"So you think Xander Thurman killed her and made it look like an overdose? Why? To protect his toddler daughter?"

"Maybe to punish Corinne for putting his child in danger?" Kat offered.

"You know, that would be an improvement in parenting from him. My most vivid childhood memory of him is being left tied to chair in a snowbound cabin as my mother's dead body decomposed in front of me."

A woman who was sitting on the stool next to Jessie choked on her drink, gave her a disgusted glare and walked to the other end of the bar. Jessie watched her go with satisfaction.

"I'm sorry," Kat said, ignoring the dustup. "I don't know the motivation or even if it was him. I'm just offering possibilities."

"You're doing fine. Don't mind my psychological brittleness," Jessie said. "What else do you have for me?"

"The rest is pretty straightforward. She was adopted by the Dorseys after about eight months in the foster care system. They lived a relatively quiet life in Van Nuys until all this happened."

"Sounds nice," Jessie said sincerely. "So no red flags?"

"I wouldn't go that far," Kat cautioned. "She had what appears to be a fairly conventional childhood. Saw a therapist for several years in her tweens, though I obviously couldn't access those records. She went to a private Catholic high school on scholarship, where she got solid, if unspectacular, grades. She was a junior, on target to graduate next year. But there were a few incidents."

Jessie took a long sip of her drink as she waited for Kat to drop the hammer.

"Information is sketchy because the academic records of minors are supposed to be sealed. But it turns out that some priests are open to unexpected financial remuneration."

"You bribed a priest?" Jessie asked incredulously, getting a dirty look from the guy two seats over.

"I made a contribution to the congregation, which I can only assume he'll pass along," Kat insisted. "Anyway, even with that, what I got was sketchy. Apparently there was an incident last year. Another girl called her a name—not clear what exactly—though it apparently had something to do with her scholarship status. Hannah grabbed the girl by the hair and dunked her head in the fountain."

"Seems fair," Jessie mused.

"She didn't let her up. Two other students had to pull her off the other girl, who was barely conscious."

"Okay, that's not great. Was she suspended?"

"Nope. Apparently the other girl was pretty despised and no one would go on the record confirming her version of what happened. Her parents threatened to sue but Hannah's folks said they'd countersue. The other girl left at the end of the school year."

"So just one incident then?"

"There was also a short story," Kat added.

"Ugh, that sounds foreboding."

"She was sent to talk to the school psychologist last fall after turning in a short story about a school shooter who dumps the bodies of her victims in the school fountain and watches 'with quiet satisfaction as the water turned crimson.' So there was that."

"How did she explain that one?" Jessie asked, starting to get a sense of Hannah and her ability to cleverly navigate complicated situations.

"There was a brief epilogue to the story in which the girl goes to juvenile detention, where she discovers Jesus. She counsels other underage detainees and starts a program to fight teenage violence. When she's finally released, she takes the program national, saving 'countless innocent lives.'"

"So she turned it into a morality tale," Jessie said.

"Technically. But the story is eight pages of vivid, detailed descriptions of slaughter. The epilogue is one paragraph long and it's kind of dry. You can tell what part she connected to. She got an 'A' by the way. The teacher said it was 'evocative' before sending her for evaluation."

"Do you have it?" Jessie asked. "Can I read it?"

"No. The priest only let me look at the file. I couldn't make copies or take photos. I guess those would have been sins."

"Anything else?"

"Nope," Kat said acidly. "Just the near-drowning of a classmate and a story imagining killing the rest of them. I'm still trying to access the notes from the school psychologist but I'm not optimistic."

"Good work, Kat. I might have to recommend you to my friends, especially if they're looking to corrupt men of the cloth or violate the privacy of teenagers."

"I'm thinking of making those my specialties," Kat said before leaning in and asking more quietly, "So what do you think? In your professional criminal profiler opinion, is she a budding serial killer?"

Jessie wondered. Years of education, training and fieldwork had taught her it wasn't as simple as that. The bulk of data on serial killers and violent serial offenders more generally suggested that most were made, not born.

In the vast majority of cases, people who killed or raped or maimed others had themselves suffered brutal trauma as children. Sometimes it was abuse. Sometimes it was being a victim of or witness to a single violent incident that resonated with them. Sometimes it was being in a perpetually violent environment. Often it was all of those things.

But that wasn't determinative. Millions of kids grow up in violent or abusive circumstances and never go on to hurt anyone. Jessie was herself an example of this—a witness to her father's abuse and eventual murder of her mother; a victim of his sadism. And yet she had gone on to fight against perpetrators like Xander Thurman. At least that was her official story.

Of course, the literature did include examples of some serial killers who had perfectly normal childhoods with loving parents and comfortable conditions. In some cases, these people were simply born with something missing. Often the capacity for great cruelty or violence correlated with an inability to feel empathy for others, which was actually measurable in the brain.

But was that just a happenstance of fate? Or was there some genetic component? Was it possible that Hannah held that mean girl's head underwater because she shared the same psychological makeup as her father? Was it possible for violent sadism to be passed down from parent to child like a family heirloom?

It seemed like a stretch to Jessie. After all, when she stepped back and tried to be objective, what was she really looking at here? At a teenage girl who wrote a provocative story and got into a fight with a girl who bad-mouthed her. How many other kids on that campus alone fit the same description? It seemed grossly unfair to stigmatize her based solely on her parentage.

And yet.

Jessie often wondered the same thing about herself. For the hundred thousandth time she asked herself if her chosen profession was genuinely about a desire to save people from monsters like her father. Or was it an excuse to be near the madness, to somehow get close without actually touching it, like a devout vegetarian chef who chooses to work at a steakhouse and gets a thrill out of watching the meat sizzle as it cooks.

"Jessie?" Kat said, snapping her back into the moment. The rush of noise the crowded bar, which had briefly faded away, returned. Her friend was watching her curiously.

"What was that again?" Jessie asked.

"I asked if you thought Hannah Dorsey was serial killer in the making?"

Jessie broke into what she hoped was a mockingly scolding smile.

"That is a wildly preposterous suggestion," she said. "And one that I'd need more than one drink to entertain. Unfortunately, I don't have the time so it'll have to wait."

She chugged the last of her drink, hopped off the stool and dropped a twenty on the bar.

"Say hi to Ryan for me," Kat said teasingly.

"I will do no such thing," Jessie replied haughtily, turning away dramatically and pretending to storm off in a huff.

She could hear Kat giggling behind her as she walked away and took both pleasure and relief in the knowledge that her friend would be left with that memory of their conversation. That was better than having her linger on whether Jessie's half-sister was a potential killer.

Jessie tried to push the subject out of her head as she walked to her car. It was 6:20 and Ryan would be cleared to leave by the time she got to the hospital. Memories of their conversation this morning made her more apprehensive than she was comfortable with.

She felt a silly grin starting to form at the corner of her lips, when an unexplainable shiver ran up her spine. She got the sudden sense that she was being watched.

Chapter Eighteen

Jessie spun around, her keys in her left hand and right hand resting on the holster of her gun. The downtown street was mostly quiet. A young couple walked toward the bar she had just left. A middle-aged man stood patiently waiting for his dog to do his business on a small patch of grass. No one was looking at her. She didn't hear anything unusual.

And then, at the far of the alley closest to her, she heard a clang, as if someone had closed or bumped into a dumpster. She stepped to her left to get a better view. But other than shadows formed by the quickly fading sun, she saw nothing.

She stood next to her car, debating whether to go down the alley, asking herself why she would even consider it, when her phone buzzed. She looked down at the message:

Patient #107939, Ryan Moses Hernandez, has been approved for conditional release. You can meet the patient at the checkout desk on level 1.

Jessie decided to leave the alley for now so that could go tease Ryan about his middle name. She hopped in the car, gave one last glance down the alley, and pulled out.

The tension was unbearable.

When she had offered to drive Ryan home, Jessie had forgotten that he didn't live near the downtown hospital where he was treated and they both worked. He lived in Venice, a good forty-five-minute drive away.

At first it was fine, as he filled her in on what the doctors had said (he *was* pushing too hard). She teased him about the middle name, Moses (his grandmother had insisted on it). And she updated him on the interview with Gavin Peck, including his mention of the other couple Taylor had been with.

Ryan wanted to go over and interview them right then. But Jessie could tell he was in no condition to conduct another interrogation and insisted they wait until tomorrow. He reluctantly agreed.

Around the halfway point to his house, they ran out of pressing topics and the awkwardness they'd managed to keep at bay all day began to set in. By the time they reached his place, no one had spoken in several minutes.

"Okay, thanks for the ride," he said as he opened the passenger door. "I'll see you tomorrow."

But as he stepped out, he grunted softly and she saw him grip the door for support.

"Don't be ridiculous," she said as she turned off the ignition and got out of the car. "You just got out of the hospital. Let me at least help you into the house."

She eased him to the front door of a small but well-maintained house on a street of similar-looking houses. When they reached the door, Jessie had a momentary flash of panic.

"Is she here?" she asked.

"No," Ryan said, fully aware of who "she" was. "Shelly is living with her sister in the valley for now. The divorce papers stipulate that once it's official, we put the house on the market and split the profits. But until then, it's mine."

He unlocked the door and she eased him in.

"Let's go to the kitchen," he said. "I haven't eaten since the chili dog and I'm starving."

"Maybe that's the real reason you had to be hospitalized," Jessie suggested.

"Don't make me laugh," he ordered, chuckling involuntarily. "It hurts."

When they got to the kitchen, he turned on the light. Jessie looked around. The room was small but well-appointed with multiple high-end appliances that must have taken years to accumulate.

"Do you want to sit down?" she asked. "I can grab you something from the fridge."

"I'd rather stand," he said. "It hurts more when I'm bent over. And I'm a little scared to let you look in my refrigerator."

"It's a risk you're going to have to take," she said as she situated him against the counter and walked across the room. "Sometimes, Ryan, we have to open the door even if we're frightened of what might be behind it."

She grasped the fridge door handle and looked back at him knowingly. He feigned cluelessness.

"I feel like you're trying to tell me something. But I also feel my stomach grumbling. So I'm not sure how to respond."

Jessie shook her head disapprovingly as she opened the door. When she did, she realized why Ryan had been apprehensive. The entire thing was comprised almost exclusively of Gatorade bottles, tortillas, hummus, peanut butter and multiple big tubs of yogurt. There were a few bottles of beer and one lonely, slightly bruised green apple.

"I don't even understand the contents of this fridge, much less have the capacity to comment on it intelligently."

"I told you not to look," he reminded her.

"I mean, come on. No milk or eggs? No meat or vegetables of any kind? It's like you're doing an experiment on your own digestive system."

"I don't shop much," he admitted. "And I eat out a lot."

"So that's where you're getting essential nutrients like leafy greens and pro-tein—when you eat out at places like Pink's Chili Dogs?"

"What's a leafy green?" he asked, straight-faced.

She smiled despite her best efforts to keep a stern expression.

"I don't even know what to give you," she said. "This hummus doesn't look safe."

"I'm good with peanut butter smeared on tortillas. Neither of those go bad, do they?"

"I guess we're about to find out," Jessie said uncertainly as she grabbed both, along with a Gatorade, and carried them over to the breakfast table.

Ryan pulled out a spoon and began to smear the peanut butter across the tortilla.

"I don't think I can stick around for this," Jessie told him. "The sight of it is going to make me lose my appetite and I haven't eaten yet tonight."

"I can split it with you," he teased.

"Hard pass. I'm going to leave you to your college dorm dinner and go find something that is actually reminiscent of real food."

She started to leave when he called her back.

"Hey, Jessie," he said. "Thanks for opening the refrigerator door for me."

She knew there was more behind the thank-you than just food and nodded, unspeaking.

"I'd walk you to the door," he said. "But I think I'd better, you know, not move so much."

"I appreciate the nod toward gallantry, even if you can't deliver on it," she replied as she walked over. "In fact, why I don't I help you to a chair? I'm not comfortable leaving you standing there. I'm worried you might pass out."

When she got to him, they did an awkward dance as she tried to find a good leverage point to support his weight as she helped move him over to the chair. Finally, she just threw his arm over her shoulder and wrapped hers tightly around his waist as they shuffled to the closet chair.

As they moved, she breathed in his not unpleasant scent—a mix of light sweat and something like nutmeg. When they got to the chair, she bent down so he could slide his arm off her shoulder. But instead of letting it drop to his side, he gently placed his hand on her hip. It took her half a second to comprehend that it wasn't for physical support.

She looked at him. They were so close that she could see tiny flecks of green in his brown eyes and individual hairs from the day-old stubble on his jaw. He looked back at her and she felt the fingers on her hip tighten.

And then, without knowing who started it, they were both leaning in, their lips lightly grazing each other and then connecting more firmly. Her eyes closed as her hands slid up to his chest. He cupped her cheeks in his palms, bringing her even closer to him. Jessie felt the stress of the day evaporate, replaced by a tingling sensation that coursed throughout her entire body.

She leaned into him more when she suddenly sensed his unsteadiness. Her eyes snapped open as she saw him reach out for support from the back of a chair. Quickly, she put her hands under his armpits and eased him into the chair.

"You okay?" she asked anxiously.

"I'm not sure what happened there," he said. "I suddenly felt dizzy."

"I have that effect on men," she said, in an attempt to keep things light.

"I guess so," he replied, still not looking totally back to normal.

"But you're okay now?" she asked.

"Yeah—I think I'll just sit for a few minutes. Once I get something in my system I should be good."

"Why don't I let you get some rest?" she suggested. "It's been a really long day and tomorrow's not going to be any easier. We have to follow up on Gavin Peck's alibi and interview the Shines."

"Yeah. I think I'm going to crash right after I eat," he said listlessly.

"Okay. I'll see you at the station in the morning then," she said.

"Sounds good," he replied as she headed for the hallway. "And Jessie, maybe tomorrow you can tell me how you get your lips so soft."

She nodded and turned to leave, unable to think of a quippy reply to that one.

CHAPTER NINETEEN

Jessie tried to act casual.

As she walked into the station the next morning, she pretended that she always wore slightly tighter than comfortable pants and mildly binding tops that pressed just a little bit extra against her chest.

No big deal. Totally professional, slightly smaller than usual outfit.

When she got to the bullpen, she saw that Ryan was already there, poring over some papers. She walked over, attempting to ignore the butterflies in her stomach. All last night and this morning, she'd tried not to obsess over what had happened, telling herself it was just a moment in time and that she shouldn't make any assumptions based on it.

They'd both been tired. Ryan was probably still under the effects of pain medication. They were both in emotionally vulnerable states. Despite all that, she couldn't help but feel a bit exhilarated. It'd been a long time since she'd had anything more than a fleeting interest in someone. And even having the capacity to be exhilarated by a romantic prospect was something she wasn't certain would ever return.

When she got to Ryan's desk, he looked up and smiled. Almost immediately, she knew they were in trouble. Despite his best effort, the smile looked forced and uncomfortable. The bags under his eyes told her he'd spent much of the night thinking about their moment too. Apparently he was feeling more apprehension than exhilaration.

"Hey you," he said, sounding overly chipper. "How's my favorite neighborhood forensic profiler this morning?"

Jessie's heart sank a bit. She didn't know what she expected, but back-slapping camaraderie wasn't at the top of her preferred list.

"She's good," she said.

He nodded...and kept nodding, seemingly unable to think of anything else to say. Apparently her doubts were nothing compared to the ones keeping him from speaking human words in English.

She tried to empathize. This was more complicated for him than for her. She'd been divorced for well over a year now. He was still in the middle of it and clearly it was raw for him. Whatever interest he had in her was probably in constant battle with the guilt he felt about the failure of his marriage.

"What are you looking at there?" she asked, letting him off the hook by nodding at the papers on his desk.

"Oh yeah, this is Gavin Peck's paternity test. He's not the father."

"Okay. That's good to know, though it doesn't eliminate him as a suspect. If he knew she was pregnant, he could still have been jealous about it. And as we know, he's not always great at controlling his emotions."

"Speaking of that," Ryan said, "he's due in court this morning for a bail hearing. I gather you want me not to oppose?"

"I promised him that if he was forthcoming, I'd put in a good word with you. Besides, I think we're better off with him out in the world. If he did this, we're more likely to see attempts to cover it up now that the pressure is on."

"Fair enough," Ryan conceded. "I'll call the court and let them know I don't oppose bail."

"That's very generous of you," Jessie said, trying to inject some playfulness back into their conversation. "And just because Gavin's not the baby daddy doesn't mean we're out of luck. If what he said is credible, we've got another contender."

"Doug Shine?" Ryan asked.

"That's right. It sounds like he and Taylor were getting up close and personal. Maybe it had, you know, consequences."

"Maybe," Ryan agreed absently, clearly not up to joke about anyone's sexual habits at the moment.

"Shall we go visit him and Mrs. Shine?" Jessie prompted.

"That sounds good," he said.

"Okay. You call the court. I just need a moment to get my stuff together and we can head out."

While he called, Jessie looked at the papers on her desk. She had the same case file as Ryan but decided she'd read it on the drive over. Quickly, she looked through her mail. She was still having all her correspondence—bills, personal letters, etc.—sent to the office. Even with her myriad security measures at the new apartment, it seemed unwise to put her name and address on any paper that could be easily accessed.

There wasn't much to look at. She had a credit card statement, a Bed, Bath & Beyond coupon, an alumni newsletter from her alma mater, USC, and a postcard with the Hollywood sign on the back. Even before she read it, Jessie knew there was something wrong with the postcard.

First of all, there was no one in her life who would send her a postcard. Second, why would someone send her one from the city in which she lived? Finally, there was no stamp or mailing address. That meant the card had been walked into the station.

Before she did anything else, Jessie grabbed a pair of evidence gloves from her drawer and snapped them on. Then she picked up the card and looked at what it said. The writing was neat and written in small block letters.

Dear Miss Jessie,

I hope that your recovery has been without incident. If it wasn't already clear, I wanted to make it so: you and your comrades are no longer the subject of my interest. I hope the attitude is reciprocal. I think it would be best if we both pursued fresh meat and fresh faces. I, for one, embrace the challenge of molding new clay. Pity your father never considered this option."

All my best,
Bolton

"You okay?" Ryan asked, standing behind her. "I thought we were heading out to talk to the Shines."

She looked up but didn't speak, merely pointing to the postcard in front of her. Ryan looked at her expression and then at the gloves on her hands. She saw in his eyes that he understood.

CHAPTER TWENTY

Jessie barely spoke.

She'd been quietly turning over the words of the postcard in her head the whole drive to the Shine house at the base of the Hollywood Hills. After several minutes of silence, Ryan tried again.

"I know it's unsettling. But maybe this is a good thing. He's saying he doesn't intend you or your comrades harm. And as one of your comrades, I find that heartening."

Jessie wasn't amused.

"Is it heartening for the 'fresh meat and fresh faces" he says he plans to go after?"

"Maybe that's just a metaphor. Crutchfield always did like to get a bit flowery in his language."

Jessie glanced over at him, unconvinced.

"Okay, maybe not a metaphor," he conceded. "But that doesn't mean we don't have options. We know the postcard had to have been dropped off yesterday for it to be in your mail this morning. Decker already had techs going through the station lobby footage from yesterday to see if we can I.D. him."

"Ryan," she replied impatiently, "we're not talking about a run of the mill criminal here. You know as well as I do that Crutchfield would have prepared for that. It's doubtful that he even dropped it off himself. He could have paid anyone on the street to do it. We don't even know who to look for."

"So we'll look at cameras outside the station too."

"You think Bolton Crutchfield was standing outside the front of Central Station to meet the person he paid to drop off my postcard, then waited to be identified before ambling off, allowing cameras to track him to his current location?"

"Wow, when you put it like that, it sounds very unlikely. I'm not sure I like your negative attitude."

Jessie didn't smile.

"I appreciate that you're trying to lighten things up so I don't freak out," she said. "But that ship has sailed. I am officially freaked."

Ryan gave up on the joking.

"I understand that. But maybe you try to press pause on the freak-out for the next hour or so. We're about to meet with potential witnesses or suspects or god knows what they are in the Jansen case. I need you in the full-on 'focused Jessie' zone."

He was right, of course. Obsessing over Bolton Crutchfield's postcard wouldn't help her get any closer to discovering the truth about Taylor Jansen's death and whether it was a murder. She owed it to the woman to uncover what had happened. And if it served as a distraction from her own problems, so be it.

She tried to shift into investigative mode, training her attention on the area they were entering. Unlike the Horsleys' neighborhood, where the homes had a more understated vibe, the homes here were a mismatched collection of houses that were gaudy, dilapidated and everything in between. Just north of the wild streets of Hollywood and south of the secluded estates of the hills, it didn't seem to know which ethos to embrace so it stole from both, sometimes on the same property.

"Looks like the Shines are a little less altruistic than the Horsleys," she said, flipping through their file as they drove.

"What, are they arms dealers or something?" Ryan asked.

"Not quite that bad," Jessie said. "Married ten years next month. No kids. Doug Shine is a real estate developer—some homes but mostly apartments and condos. Claire is self-employed. It looks like she sells vitamin supplements for one of those multi-level marketing companies."

"Either of them have a record?"

"Nope, clean as a whistle," Jessie answered. "But neither of them has saved children with life-threatening heart conditions either."

"Then let's lock 'em up!" Ryan shouted as he pulled onto their street.

Jessie appreciated the moment of levity, however brief. Still, they were going to need to work out this tension between them soon. Neither her personal nor professional life could handle the pins and needles.

They pulled up to a house that was neither gaudy nor dilapidated. It was old, maybe even historically so, which meant about a hundred years in Los Angeles. But it had been updated and modernized in subtle ways that didn't detract from the style of the original. They included a faux-wood automatic garage, an addition that blended seamlessly with the original structure, and solar panels that looked like decorative skylights.

They parked in front and headed for the front door. Jessie couldn't help but try to guess which window Gavin had peeked through. As they approached, the garage door opened to reveal two cars. It seemed both Shines were still home. A moment later a man stepped into view.

He was just as Gavin had described him—in his mid-thirties, tall and thin, but clearly in good shape. He had wavy black hair that was currently slicked back and tied in a short ponytail. Jessie felt immediate revulsion at the sight. He was handsome in an overly sculpted way, with a chin that seemed chiseled from tan granite.

He looked at the car blocking his exit, then saw the people on his doorstep.

"Can I help you?" he asked in a tone that suggested he wasn't interested in doing so.

"You bet," Ryan exclaimed with unexpected energy. "Are you Doug Shine, the noted real estate mogul?"

"I guess," Doug said, not sure if he was being mocked. "Who are you?"

"Damn glad to meet you, Doug. I'm Ryan Hernandez and this is Jessie Hunt. We work for the city and we wanted to talk to you and your wife for a few minutes if we might."

Jessie wasn't sure what tactic Ryan was employing. Whatever it was, she was both confused and intrigued and decided to watch it play out.

"You can't just come on my property, claim you 'work for the city' and expect me to invite you in. What is this about exactly?" he demanded.

The sound of a door unlocking stopped the conversation. A moment later the front door opened and a trim, blond thirty-something woman stepped out. Gavin had described Claire Shine as skinny, giving the impression of frailty. But looking at her now, Jessie thought that was only in comparison to Taylor's more muscled frame. Claire was wiry and taut-looking, like an athlete who had retired but still worked out regularly.

"Everything okay, hon?" she asked, saccharine sweet.

"I don't know, sweetums," he said, equally sugary. "We have a couple of strangers who want to talk to us. They say they're from the city, whatever that means."

"It means," Ryan said, the chummy tone now gone from his voice as he pulled out his badge, "that we're here on LAPD business and we have some questions for you. It means that you're going to be late for whatever meeting you were headed to. So evicting tenants and raising rents is going to have to be put on hold for a bit. Now, shall we have this chat in the house or here in the front yard where your neighbors might see, or worse, hear it? Or should we have it back at the station?"

"Why don't you folks come on inside and we'll see if we can't get you some coffee," Claire said before her husband could reply. He looked over at her, annoyed, and got back a withering glare in response.

"Yeah, come on in," he finally said. "We're always happy to help out the boys in blue, or whatever unusual shade of gray that jacket is."

Much to Jessie's relief, Ryan decided to let that one go. They followed Claire into the house, which immediately opened onto a massive living room with a view of the hills behind them.

"I'm sorry I missed the introductions," Claire said as she indicated for them to sit down on the plush leather sofa. "I'm Claire Shine, Doug's wife."

Jessie noticed her wince slightly as she said it, as if it pained her a bit. Out of the corner of her eye, she also saw Doug stiffen at the description.

"I'm Jessie Hunt," she said, deciding to keep her observation to herself for now. "I'm a forensic profiler with LAPD. That charmer is Detective Ryan Hernandez. Your name has come up in an investigation and we thought it prudent to speak to you to see if you could be of assistance."

"Are we in some kind of trouble?" Claire asked, her brow furrowed.

"At this point, we're just gathering information," Jessie said in her most reassuring voice. "No one is in trouble. We're just piecing things together and hope you can add to the overall picture. Are you amenable to that?"

The couple looked at each other hesitantly. Jessie could tell they were torn between wanting nothing to do with this and not wanting to look like they had something to hide.

"We'll help," Doug said reluctantly. "Though it would be nice to know what this is about."

"Do you know a woman named Taylor Jansen?" Ryan asked forcefully and without preamble.

They looked at each other again, trading apprehensive glances. Claire spoke first.

"She was my personal trainer until a couple of months ago."

"Why isn't she now?" Ryan pressed.

Both Shines looked at the floor, like students called into the principal's office. After a moment, Doug looked up.

"It's hard to be very forthcoming when we don't know what this is about. You're asking us very personal questions."

"Really?" Jessie asked innocently. "Is it that personal to ask why you don't use a particular trainer anymore?"

Claire Shine looked back at her with narrowed, unblinking eyes. It was clear that she knew what they were getting at. She seemed to be weighing how cooperative to be. They stared at each other for a brief eternity, sizing each other up. Finally she spoke.

"It's only personal in the sense that Taylor is the reason Doug and I are getting divorced."

Chapter Twenty One

Doug had a sudden coughing fit. Ryan's eyes went wide. Jessie was shocked, though not surprised. Now the nasty looks between the couple made more sense.

"Care to elaborate?" she asked as if this was the answer she expected.

"Maybe you don't," Doug suggested to her desperately.

"It's too late, Boo," Claire said derisively. "They obviously already know. So we may as well come clean."

"I think that's the smart move," Jessie agreed, curious to learn just what "coming clean" meant.

"So someone clearly told you that we were . . . seeing her, if you want to be delicate about it," Claire said.

"We had heard that," Jessie confirmed. "So both of you were involved with her?"

"That's right. At first, it was just me. Then it became a group thing."

"How did things . . . evolve?" Ryan asked.

"She was my trainer and briefly in my down line. I sell nutritional supplements and encourage others to do the same. She joined up very briefly before deciding it wasn't for her. But spending time outside of the gym was stimulating. We had a flirty connection. And when she broke up with her boyfriend, I made a pass at her. At first she was scandalized, but then not so much. So we hooked up. After a few get-togethers, I asked if she'd mind if Doug joined in. She was curious. That turned into outright enthusiasm. She was even open to what I'll delicately call 'rough play.' But after about a month, she called it off."

"Why?" Ryan asked.

Once again, the Shines exchanged a look that suggested they weren't sure how honest to be. This time it was Doug who spoke up.

"Our marriage was already on the rocks for a while before we met Taylor. At first, she gave us a shot of excitement and things started looking up. But after a few weeks, the issues we already had cropped up again. We each started to get jealous of the time she spent with the other person. We resented each other for getting her off."

Jessie and Ryan exchanged a glance that indicated they were both entering uncharted territory.

"I thought this threesome thing was all about being open and setting aside petty emotions like jealousy," Ryan said.

"Yeah," Doug replied. "That's the way it's supposed to work, but not so much for us. We both like the thrill of having someone else in the mix. But the truth is, we're also both competitive, selfish people. So long-term, there were always going to be issues."

"But I assume you had done this sort of thing before?" Jessie said. "Why did it fall apart this time and not the others?"

For the first time since they'd arrived, Jessie watched both Shines smile genuinely. Claire explained.

"Because Taylor was different. She had this allure, this 'attack every moment of life' charisma that was somehow sexy and innocent at the same time."

"Yeah," Doug agreed. "All the other people we brought in were just props in our attempts to satisfy ourselves. But with Taylor, we wanted to satisfy her. We wanted to make her happy. And pretty quickly, we started to view each other as obstacles to that."

"After a while, she got turned off by the negativity," Claire added. "So she said she didn't want to continue. And training with her after that would have been slightly awkward."

Doug picked up from there.

"After she left, without anything to distract us from how much we hated each other, we decided to end the charade and make it official."

"But you're both still here," Ryan noted.

"We sleep in separate bedrooms," Claire said.

"It's just more practical and cost-effective to both live here until the divorce is final," Doug added. "Even then, we might continue for a while longer."

"We'll see about that," Claire replied acidly.

"Do you blame Taylor for the end of your marriage?" Jessie asked, trying not to attach too much obvious weight to the question.

Again, a shared uneasy look passed between the estranged couple. After several long seconds, Claire answered for them both.

"I blame us."

"So we've answered all your questions," Doug quickly countered. "Now can you please tell us what this is about? Did Taylor do something wrong?"

Now it was Jessie's and Ryan's turn to exchange an uncomfortable look. After a moment, she gave him the half-nod she knew he'd understand—once again he should tell the couple the truth so she could watch their reactions. He nodded back slightly.

"I'm sorry to say that Taylor is dead," he said.

The Shines gasped in unison.

"What happened?" Claire asked.

"We're still trying to determine that," Ryan told her. "That's why we're speaking to everyone she interacted with recently, to get a better picture of her life."

"But we haven't interacted with her recently," Doug pointed out. Jessie was taken by how quickly his shock turned to defensiveness.

"When was the last time you saw her?" Ryan asked.

"I couldn't tell you exactly," Doug said. "But many weeks, maybe even a few months."

Jessie looked at Claire, who was notably silent.

"Do you agree with that timetable?" she asked.

Claire looked up, red-faced.

"I might have seen her more recently than that," she admitted quietly.

"What!" Doug shouted.

"When?" Jessie asked.

"A couple of weeks ago," Claire muttered. "I ran into her at the market and we got to talking and one thing led to another and . . . it was just one time. She's hard to give up."

"You didn't know anything about this?" Ryan asked the clearly seething husband.

"No," he spat. "Or I would have pushed to divorce the bitch earlier."

"Hey," Ryan cautioned.

"We weren't together anymore, Doug," Claire screamed back. "You don't have the right to get jealous anymore. I can screw whoever I want. Just be happy I didn't bring her back to the house, you greasy-haired caveman."

"Okay," Jessie interrupted. "So you two clearly have some issues to work out. But we're not going to do that here and now. What we need from you are your whereabouts on Monday from about noon to four the next morning."

The Shines stared daggers at each other before Claire finally pulled out her phone and looked at her calendar. After a few seconds, Doug did the same.

"I was at supplement soirees all day," Claire announced.

"I'm sorry, what?" Jessie asked.

"They're like Tupperware parties," Claire explained. "Only for the supplements I offer. I give a presentation, show videos, provide free samples, and sign people up to join the program or my down line. I had three soirees that day."

"Okay," Ryan said, clearly stunned that these parties were an actual thing that people did. "And you, Mr. Shine?"

"I had a few meetings in the morning," he said, studying his screen. "Then I spent the afternoon visiting various properties and checking in with site managers."

"And that evening?" Jessie asked.

"We went to the opening of a new club on Highland Avenue," Doug said. "A friend of mine owns it. No one else knows about the divorce yet so we wanted to keep up appearances."

"Okay," Ryan said. "We're going to need you to provide detailed timetables of your locations during that stretch along with anyone who can verify your whereabouts. We'd also like you to provide a DNA sample, Mr. Shine."

"Why?" he demanded indignantly.

"Because Taylor was pregnant at the time of her death," Ryan revealed. "We're trying to determine who the father is."

"But Doug always used protection," Claire insisted." We're kinky but we're not stupid."

Jessie noticed that Doug was silent.

"Do you have something to add, Mr. Shine?" she asked.

He waited a long time before responding.

"I didn't always use protection," he admitted softly.

"What?" Claire said incredulously. "Yes you did. I helped you—don't you remember?"

He paused, clearly sensing that what he was about to say wouldn't be well-received.

"There may have been a few times that Taylor and I got together without you."

Ryan looked over at Jessie with an expression she'd never seen before—a combination of genuine shock mixed with an intense effort to stifle a laugh. She felt just like he looked. It was as if they'd just stepped into an episode of a bad soap opera. Claire stared at her not-for-long husband for several seconds before responding.

"You...are a pig," she said simply and without emotion.

"Right back at you," he sneered.

"So we'd like that sample today," Ryan interjected, hoping to stave off whatever storm was brewing.

"I'll get right on that," Doug said, not looking at anyone in particular.

"We're going to leave now," Jessie said, talking as much to stave off the tension as to convey information. "But if the sample, those activity logs, and the alibi witnesses aren't provided by noon, we'll have to send officers back. That gives you several hours, so I'd start on it now. Reconstructing a daily timeline can be harder than you think."

Neither of the Shines spoke as Jessie and Ryan showed themselves out. They hurried to the door, happy to leave the impending ice storm behind them.

Chapter Twenty Two

"This information would have been a little more helpful an hour ago!" Ryan bellowed into the phone as they drove back to the station.

They had only been back in the car for five minutes after the Shine interview when they got a call from Reggie Toney in the Organized Crime Unit.

"I only just heard that you're meeting with Doug Shine this morning," Reggie had said.

"We just left his place," Ryan had replied. "Why?"

"That's too bad," Reggie said apologetically. "You probably didn't know we're looking at him for mob ties."

This was around the time Ryan blew up. After the outburst, he regrouped enough to ask for an explanation. Reggie provided it, seemingly unbothered by just having been yelled at.

"We think Shine uses some of his rental properties to launder money for the Propov crime syndicate based out of Russia. The trick is that some of the properties are totally legit and the ones that aren't go through multiple shell companies. It's a nightmare to trace."

Ryan visibly shook himself, as if trying to physically exorcise his frustration at having been left in the dark.

"Do you think that if we pushed him from that angle," he began, "he might shake something loose on this suspicious death we're investigating?"

"That's the main reason I wanted to reach out. I specifically *don't* want you to talk to him about the laundering stuff. We've been on him for almost a year and haven't been able to nail anything down yet. He's very careful, even without being aware that we're tracking him. But he's also strangely reckless. He went to a club opening for one of these mobbed up guys just last night, which shows he's not concerned about appearances."

"That's not the only way he's reckless," Jessie muttered under her breath.

"What's that?" Reggie asked.

"Nothing," Ryan said, frowning at her. "Anything else we should know?"

"Yeah, as long as I'm laying all my cards on the table, we think his wife is a drug dealer too."

"What?" Jessie couldn't help but exclaim.

"Bold, right?' "Reggie said, chuckling slightly. "We think she uses the supplement business as a front to deal black market opioids for her husband's business partners. She doesn't sell anything herself. But she picks a few prospects from her down line who she can manipulate. Usually, it's women who are desperate for the extra money and willing to take the hit if it goes bad. We're hesitant to try to turn any of the women without an iron-clad case against them for fear they'll warn Claire Shine."

"Wow," Jessie said, impressed. "I have to say, they had me snowed. I had no suspicion about any of this. I thought they were just a bitter couple who liked threesomes."

"I'm sorry," Reggie said. "What was that?"

"We'll get back to you, Reg," Ryan said, before hanging up. "Thanks for the heads-up."

"Makes you wonder," he said after they'd sat in silence for several seconds, "if they're that good at hiding multiple illicit activities over many months, how challenging would it be to get rid of a troublesome trainer and act stunned hearing about it later?"

"Good point," Jessie agreed. "Though we don't really have much of a motive for them."

"Maybe Taylor stumbled onto some of their illegality," he suggested. "Or maybe she told Doug he was the baby's father and he reacted poorly."

"I guess we'll have more clarity on that in a few hours," Jessie said absently.

Something Ryan had just said caused an odd stirring in her mind, as if she was missing something important but couldn't quite put her finger on it. Try as she might, she couldn't quite nail it down.

"What I need clarity on," Ryan said, interrupting her thoughts, "is this timeline. If we're going to figure this out, we need to get it straight in our heads."

Jessie decided to let the slippery thought darting around her brain go for now in the hopes that it would return on its own.

"Okay," she said. "We know Jessie formally broke up with Gavin about three months ago, right?"

"Yes," Ryan agreed. "And according to both him and the Shines, she took up with them within a week of that. But their 'special time' together only lasted about a month before they alienated her with their general unpleasantness."

"Right," Jessie continued. "That fits with when Meadow Horsley said she took up with Taylor, around two months ago."

"And it sounds like that was petering out too," Ryan noted. "If Meadow is to be believed, when Taylor stopped returning her calls and texts, she thought it was because she'd lost interest."

"But," Jessie reminded him, "we know that by then, Taylor was probably already dead."

"Yes," Ryan concurred. "But if Meadow didn't know that and she thought Taylor was freezing her out, it suggests that she suspected things were winding down. It seems like Taylor had a pattern. Whether it was monogamous relationships or open ones with several partners, she didn't stick around for long."

"Just like Gavin said—he wasn't enough for her. It sounds like not even multiple couples were either."

When they got back to the station, Decker was waiting for them. Jessie assumed he'd had the parking garage officer call him when they arrived because they hadn't even entered the building when he opened the door to greet them.

"Captain Decker," Ryan said with unconvincing enthusiasm. "We were just coming to see you."

"That works out perfectly," Decker replied tersely, "since I was just coming to pull you two off the case."

CHAPTER TWENTY THREE

Jessie was proud of herself for not yelling.

The same could not be said for Detective Hernandez, who was lucky he wasn't suspended for his initial verbal reaction, which included a variety of profanities that Jessie hadn't ever heard in a professional setting. To his credit, Captain Decker waited until they were all in his office with the door closed before he responded.

"I'm going to chalk up that outburst to you still being a little out of it after your hospitalization yesterday, which you both neglected to mention to me."

Jessie was about to do a verbal tap dance when Ryan jumped in.

"That's my fault, sir, as was my inappropriate eruption earlier," he said, after having a few minutes to cool off. "I wasn't forthcoming with Jessie and gave her the impression that I was fine. She wouldn't have had cause to update you because I withheld that information from her as well."

"Is that accurate, Ms. Hunt?" Captain Decker asked, turning to her and fixing his beady, hawk-like eyes on hers.

She chose her words carefully, hoping they would satisfy him.

"I was not fully aware of the nature of Detective Hernandez's condition."

"Because I neglected to make her aware, sir." Ryan insisted. "Having said that, I got the all-clear from the doctors and feel fine now. I just pushed a little harder than I should have is all."

"I want to see that all-clear in writing, Hernandez," Decker said, clearly still skeptical. "Regardless, you're off the case. The gang shooting is falling into line and we have people available now. I'll have Trembley take over. It sounds like there's not much left to do anyway."

"That's not true, Captain," Jessie said forcefully. "We're still verifying the alibis of five potential suspects and waiting on final confirmation of cause of death. There's more to do here, sir."

Decker gave her his most exasperated sigh.

"Let me ask you something, Hunt. Do you have a primary suspect? Do any of these five people have a plausible motive?"

Jessie paused before answering.

"It's too early to be sure," she finally said.

"That's a no," Decker barked back at her. "Do you even have credible evidence that suggests this is actually a murder and not a suicide or accidental death?"

"All of those scenarios are in play, Captain," she said, aware she was not winning him over.

"That's a no, too," he seethed. "So you have no credible suspects and no hard evidence that a crime has even been committed. Is that a fair assessment of the situation?"

"Captain, it's not that simple. Some of the facts have to be teased out . . ."

"I don't like teases, Hunt. I like facts and motives and evidence, all of which seem to be in short supply here. Give me one good reason to let you two continue to pursue this case."

"It'll keep us out of trouble," Ryan blurted out, making an argument that even Jessie didn't understand.

"What?" Decker asked.

"You want us both to avoid taking risks, right? If what you say is true and we're pursuing a crime that didn't happen, then how much safer can we be?"

Decker looked at him, flabbergasted.

"At least give us until the end of the day, Captain," Ryan pleaded. "If we don't bring you something substantive by then, fine—take us off the case. Put Trembley on it. Or don't put anyone on it. We won't fight you. But at least let us pull these last few threads. Please?"

Decker swiveled his head between the two of them. Jessie put on her most forlorn expression and hoped that her captain would be susceptible. His face was inscrutable. He seemed to be doing mental calculations in his head.

"End of business today," he finally muttered. "You bring me hard evidence of an actual crime and a legitimate potential suspect or you're getting pulled and I'm having Trembley put this thing to bed. Are we clear?"

Jessie nodded.

"Thank you, Captain," Ryan added.

"Get out of my office," Decker replied. "You're wasting time."

They did as they were told. As they walked over to their desks, Jessie leaned in and murmured, "Good save."

"Thanks," he replied. "Let's make the most of it."

"Right," she said, pausing briefly before adding something that had been eating at her since they were last at their desks earlier that morning. "Maybe when we get a spare moment, we can discuss that other thing?"

"What other thing?" he asked, though she could tell from the way he didn't look straight at her that he knew what she was talking about.

"The thing that happened last night and how you've been super awkward ever since," she reminded him.

"Oh, that."

"Yeah, that."

"I definitely want to talk to you," he said, speaking much faster than usual. "But let's save it for after work, okay? I have a feeling that's it's going to be a longer conversation than we have time for now. Let's just stay focused on the case. Is that all right?"

"Sure," she said, managing not to add what she really wanted to say.

That sounds ominous.

Everyone's alibi checked out.

At least initially, that is. With papers strewn out over their two desks, Jessie and Ryan spent the next hour poring over the GPS data from all five main suspects' cars and phones, as well as calling everyone on their list of alibi witnesses. In each case, they bounced theories and ideas off each other in the hope that some clear scenario would emerge.

The Horsleys' movements were very well established, with tracking data showing them going to work together on Monday morning after leaving Solstice Fitness. After that, multiple witnesses placed them at the hospital all day up until they returned home together that evening, which GPS data again verified.

It would have been hard to manipulate all that data, especially for a couple that didn't seem to have any expertise in that area. There was also tracking data of them driving to and from Santa Barbara on Tuesday, along with phone records, though Tuesday now seemed to be outside the time of death window.

Gavin Peck's location also seemed to be straightforward. His phone, vehicle and computer data all suggested that he was working at his small house for most of the day before heading to his gym in the late afternoon. There was video footage of him arriving at the gym, on the workout floor and leaving later that night.

All of that seemed credible. But unlike the Horsleys, Jessie was less confident that Gavin's information during the day was genuine. He was, after all, a web designer. It wasn't outside his skill set to manipulate his computer so it looked like he was working from home while he was doing it remotely. If he somehow got a ride to and from Taylor's place, it might seem that he was home while he was out doing her harm.

Of course, a guy his size was hard to miss and there was no surveillance footage from the area around her apartment of anyone who looked like him. That didn't mean much because there were so few working security cameras near Taylor's complex anyway. As a result, there were so many blind spots that even a completely naked person, if he took a certain route, could have walked from the street outside to her place without being recorded.

Just in the last hour, the Shines had submitted their movements from Monday along with a DNA sample from Doug, which would provide results in a few hours. And for all their questionable legal circumstances, they too had fairly ironclad alibis. Phone and vehicle GPS data backed up their claims about their whereabouts. Claire had almost two dozen alibi witness spread out among her three supplement soirees. Doug's data showed him bouncing from place to place and calls verified that he met with the people he claimed to have met with.

But if he was mobbed up and asked for help from his benefactors, could they have pressured people to lie about the meetings to give him cover? Was it conceivable that some minion might take his phone and drive his car around while another one gave him a ride to Taylor's to take her out? Or could some professional mob killer have done it on his behalf, making it look like an accident? The permutations were seemingly limitless. Jessie was getting a headache and that was before they even considered motives.

"Claire may have said they blamed themselves for their marriage falling apart, but she wasn't all that convincing to me," Jessie noted. "I could easily see her blaming Taylor for tearing open the cracks that were already there. And I'm not convinced she didn't know that Taylor and Doug were secretly sleeping together."

"But you could say the same thing about Doug," Ryan countered. "He seemed very focused on appearances, wanting them to go to that club opening together. His marriage falling apart could have serious repercussions for his business, or at least for appearances, which seem to be important to him. I could envision him taking that out on Taylor. And if you throw an unwanted pregnancy in the mix, that adds even more motive."

Jessie sat quietly for a minute, unable to think of an obvious counter to his point. Her instinct was that Claire was more manipulative than her husband, but that didn't necessarily mean anything. Manipulative didn't mean murderer.

"What about Gavin?" she said, deciding to move on for now. "He's a walking ball of motive. He essentially admitted to stalking. The jealousy was right there on the surface."

"Right," Ryan agreed excitedly. "And you could tell his ego was bruised. And after looking at the video of your interrogation of him, he seemed to think it was a failure on his part that his ex-girlfriend started exploring her sexuality right after their breakup."

"Although," Jessie noted, tempering her enthusiasm for the theory, "one would have expected him to do something drastic right after finding out. It seems less likely that he'd come after her three months later, without a precipitating incident."

"That we know of," Ryan added.

"Right," she said, her mind already drifting to the next potential subjects. "So what about the Horsleys? What might have set one of them off?"

"They both have stellar professional reputations," Ryan mused. "Maybe Taylor threatened to reveal the nature of their relationship? Maybe she took secret photos and blackmailed them? It's not a stretch to think a renowned pediatric heart surgeon wouldn't want his sexual peccadilloes getting out."

"That's possible. But we don't have a shred of evidence that she was blackmailing either of them. And if she did that, one would think she'd have done it with the Shines too. Someone would have let something slip. Besides, I just don't see Taylor as the blackmailing type."

"But did you see her as the S&M, threesome type?" Ryan asked.

"Touché."

They fell into silence, ignoring the hubbub of the bullpen as they both pondered all the varying permutations.

"You know," Jessie finally said, "maybe we're forcing it. We've honed in on these suspects. But she had other clients. Maybe we need start fresh and see if we're missing someone."

"Or," Ryan said, sounding like he didn't want to offer this alternative, "maybe these alibis all check out for a reason. Maybe we're having trouble nailing down a motive for that same reason."

"What's that?"

"Maybe *no one* did this to Taylor. What if the original theory is right and it was just an unfortunate accident? A woman took too many sleeping pills and never woke up. It wouldn't be the first time."

"Maybe," Jessie allowed, though everything inside her told her that wasn't the case.

"We could tell Decker we're handing the case off to Trembley," Ryan said reluctantly. "Part of me thinks we're clinging to this murder hypothesis because we both need a case to solve. I don't like to admit it, but I can't deny the thought has occurred to me."

The truth was, Jessie had the same idea on more than one occasion over the last hour. Was she really getting justice for a victimized woman? Or was she just using Taylor Jansen to work out her own issues? Did she *need* this to be a crime?

She stewed in those doubts for a while before finally looking up at Ryan and giving him her answer.

"I'm not ready to give up yet."

Chapter Twenty Four

S o they didn't.

But after another unproductive hour of reviewing communications with other clients, they began to reconsider. It was early afternoon and Decker's ticking clock was running out of time. Jessie was just about to propose that they ask Reggie from Organized Crime who the Propov family's favorite assassins for hire were when Hundley from the medical tech team walked in and handed over a lab analysis.

"I have no idea what this means," Ryan said.

Hundley gave an officious snort.

"It means Doug Shine isn't a genetic match," he said, then spoke in his best Darth Vader voice. "He's not the father."

Ryan gave him a dead-eyed stare.

"That's not very funny, Hundley. We're talking about a possible murder here."

Hundley slinked off sheepishly. When he was out of earshot, Ryan turned to Jessie.

"That was actually pretty funny," he whispered. "I just didn't want him to get cocky."

"I'm happy that you kept him in his place," Jessie said impatiently. "More importantly, it looks like the primary motive for Doug Shine to want to silence Taylor just went out the window."

Ryan's grin faded.

"I think we may be on fumes here," he said grudgingly.

Jessie was inclined to agree. If Doug wasn't concerned about paternity, the most credible justification for him to want to get rid of Taylor was gone. He just didn't seem like the kind of guy who would be that upset about his sexual proclivities getting out. Then again, Jessie had to admit that he didn't seem like the kind of guy who would be broken up about a paternity allegation either. He might even wear it as a sign of his prowess. After all, his reputation wasn't built on his human decency, it was built on his ability to sell.

And then, as if a magician pulled back the curtain of her mind, something clicked. The thought she'd been circling earlier in the day, the one she couldn't quite nail down, came to her fully formed.

"You know," she said, turning to Ryan, "I think we've been a little too hands off when it comes to this whole 'BDSM' thing."

"I'm sorry?" he replied, his eyes wide and his mouth agape.

"Not *us*," she said acidly. "You've been an unholy mess after one damn kiss. I'm saying in regard to these couples. We've just assumed because they were so upfront about what they're into that there's no reason to doubt them."

"What's wrong with that assumption?" he asked, relieved that this was about the case and not them.

"We already know it's not true," Jessie said flatly. "Just this morning we found out that Taylor was sleeping with both Shines without the other's knowledge and you saw that the revelation didn't go over well."

"Okay. I'm still not following."

Jessie realized her brain was operating faster than her words and tried to slow down.

"If the Shines lied," she said, "the Horsleys might have too, or at least one of them. Cal said that he only ever watched, never participated. But what if that got old after a while? What if he did eventually spend some private time with Taylor without his wife's knowledge? That's not the sort of thing he'd tell us, at least not in front of her. And we already know Taylor is open to the concept. So if Cal Horsley was secretly having sex with her, maybe he's the father of her child."

"Maybe," Ryan conceded. "But don't you think he'd just try to pay her off to terminate the pregnancy or go away?"

"Who's to say he didn't? And who's to say it didn't go badly? If she refused, he'd be pretty frustrated. And that's a motive for a guy who is viewed as a hero to so many children and their parents."

Ryan rolled the theory around in his head before turning back to her.

"Are you thinking what I'm thinking?" he asked.

"That depends," Jessie replied. "Are you thinking we should go over to the hospital right now and ask him to take a paternity test and see how he reacts?"

"You *are* thinking what I'm thinking," he said, a broad smile on his face.

They agreed to meet up at the car after a quick bathroom break. Jessie was just walking out to the garage when she got a call on her cell. It was Kat. She picked up immediately.

"I've got some info," her friend said without any kind of introductory greeting.

Jessie appreciated her directness.

"Tell me," she replied.

"Do you recall how I said I might be able to access some notes from the . . . chats a person of interest had?"

Jessie immediately understood that Kat was talking about Hannah's sessions with the school psychologist and that she was being cryptic as an extra precaution.

"I do," she assured her.

"Well, I was successful . . . kind of."

"What does that mean?" Jessie wanted to know.

"I was able to secure a brief summary from the notes of the first time our person of interest went for a chat last year, after the fountain incident I described to you. It was given to me verbally. Do you want to hear what it says now or wait until we can meet in person?"

"I'm gonna give you one guess, Kat," Jessie said sharply.

"Here we go then," Kat said, unsurprised by the answer. She began reciting what she'd been told:

"Patient refuses to engage regarding current emotional status. However, patient did acknowledge regular difficulty sleeping and repeated nightmares involving the death of her mother and a 'shadow man' who was there the night she died. When asked if she has 'shadow man' nightmares in other contexts beyond her mother's death, she was non-responsive. Prescription to follow. Patient shut down completely at any attempt to address anger management issues. Despite her trauma, Patient is high-functioning with an impressive ability to compartmentalize pain and loss, perhaps to her long-term detriment. Patient agreed to attend subsequent sessions only after being informed that it was required to avoid expulsion."

"That's it," Kat said.

"Really? That's all there is?"

"That's all there is from that summary. But my source says that was the most illuminating note in the file. After that, she basically shut down completely. She never addressed her mother's death again. She denied any recollection of the 'shadow man.' Apparently she did just enough to get cleared by the psycholo . . . interviewer and nothing more."

"Okay. Well, thanks. This is more than I knew before."

"What do you think?" Kat asked.

"I think this girl was seriously messed up long before what happened two months ago. And I can't imagine how lost she is now."

"You know you can't see her, right, Jessie?" Kat said.

"Where is that coming from?"

"Because I know you," Kat said. "And I can hear in your voice that you are aching to talk to her. Don't. The whole point of involving me is to protect you. Don't screw that up."

"Don't worry. Thanks, Kat. Talk later," she said, hanging up without waiting for a response.

She pointedly did not agree *not* to talk to Hannah. That was because if she had, she would have been lying to her friend.

Chapter Twenty Five

R yan was suspicious right away.

Jessie could sense it in him the second she insisted on driving. She was usually ambivalent about it and only made a big deal if he was eating or pissed off. He was neither right now and his sideways glance told her he was curious.

But he said nothing and hopped in the passenger seat. He didn't say anything when they took a different route to the hospital from the one she knew he would have expected. Nor did he comment when she said she needed to make a quick pit stop. It was only when they pulled up in front of the ranch-style house with the hammock on the porch in the quiet residential neighborhood that he finally asked a question.

"What are we doing here?"

"I realized we were in the neighborhood where the girl Xander Thurman kidnapped is living with her foster family. I thought I'd check in as long as we're so close."

Jessie looked over at him and felt sure that she could read his thoughts. They were likely along the lines of "the only reason we're so close is because you drove out of your way to get here." But he refrained from any snark.

"This is the girl you rescued—Hannah something?"

"Right, Hannah Dorsey. She actually rescued me. Without her quick thinking, I wouldn't be here."

"So now she's living with a foster family?"

"Yeah. I've been meaning to check in on her—see how she's doing. But I wanted to give her some space. I figure two months is long enough. What do you think?"

"Jessie," he said carefully, clearly sensing that he was dealing with a loaded question, "I don't pretend to be any kind of expert on this sort of thing. If you think she's ready, then she probably is."

Jessie wondered if he'd feel the same way if he had all the information, including the fact that they were half-sisters and that she was there in part to suss out just how damaged her sibling was.

"Yeah—I think so too," was all she said in response. "Mind staying here? I don't want to overwhelm her."

"No problem. But don't take too long. Remember, we're on a ticking clock here."

Jessie nodded, got out of the car, and strode up the walkway to the front door. She was about to knock when she heard a voice to her right.

"They don't like solicitors."

She looked over to see Hannah lying in a hammock tied to two porch posts, a copy of *The Catcher in the Rye* resting on her chest.

"I'm not a solicitor," Jessie said. "I work for the LAPD. I'm actually here to see you."

Hannah, who until that point had been splayed out languorously, sat upright.

Jessie barely recognized her as the girl from that night. Her sandy blonde hair, shoulder length the night of the attack, was now in a pixie cut. Her green eyes, which had been puffy and red from crying, were now clear and sparkling. Jessie couldn't help but notice they were the same as her own.

"You're the one," Hannah said sharply. "From that night. From when . . . it happened."

"Yes. My name's Jessie. And you're Hannah, right?"

Hannah stared at her for a long second before responding.

"Uh-huh," she finally said, before adding, "But you knew that."

"I did," Jessie admitted, not wanting to lie to this girl any more than necessary. "I've been wanting to check in on you for a while. But I was worried it might bring up bad memories."

"The memories are there no matter what, Jessie," she replied, using the name like a weapon.

"That's true," Jessie agreed. "But if you deal with them properly, sometimes they fade a little bit."

"Has that happened for you, Jessie?" Hannah challenged.

This girl wasn't afraid to be direct. Jessie found it both refreshing and a little unsettling.

"Not as much as I'd like," she conceded. "It's too fresh right now. But I've been through some pretty ugly stuff in the past and I find that time does make things a little…hazy."

Hannah swung her long legs over the hammock and put her feet flat on the porch floor. She studied Jessie for several seconds and the older woman felt like she was being subjected to a human bullshit detector.

"What 'ugly stuff' have you been through, Jessie?" she asked, again bludgeoning her with her own name.

This was the moment when Jessie would normally deflect or turn things back on her subject. But that didn't seem like an option now. First, Hannah would likely pick up on her tactic and decide to shut her out. But second, and far more surprising, she didn't want to. She felt the sudden strong urge to be honest with this girl, at least as much as she reasonably could.

"My adoptive parents were murdered too. Not that long ago actually. They were older."

Hannah looked at her hard.

"I'm sorry," she said after a few seconds. "Were you there?"

"No. But I was there when my mother was murdered by my father. I was six then."

Hannah's eyes opened wide and for the first time, her jaded façade seemed to drop.

"Really?"

"Really. That one never goes away. I still have nightmares, though not as often or as vivid as I used to."

"Did they catch him?" Hannah asked. "Your father?"

Jessie looked at the girl, unsure how to possibly answer that question the way it needed to be answered.

"Eventually," she finally said.

"Hannah," a female voice called out from inside. "Is there someone out there with you?"

Hannah started to answer but stopped when Jessie shook her head.

"I'm not technically supposed to be here," she said quietly. "Not until the case is formally closed. I just felt like I owed it to you to see how you are. But I could get in trouble at work."

The front door opened and a woman stepped out. She was in her late thirties with prematurely gray hair and creases along her eyes that suggested she didn't get many couple's massages.

"Who are you?" she demanded.

Jessie looked at Hannah. For the first time since Jessie had stepped onto the porch, the girl smiled at her. She had a mischievous gleam in her eye.

"She's just looking for directions to the closest liquor store," she lied convincingly. "She's going to some kind of house party nearby and forgot to bring a gift. But I told her I have no idea where a liquor store would be, what with me being a minor and all."

The woman looked from Hannah to Jessie, clearly bewildered.

"Why would you ask a kid where to get alcohol?' she demanded.

Jessie tried to ignore Hannah, whose smile had cracked into a wide grin.

"That's a good question," she agreed. "The truth is . . . I didn't realize she was underage when I pulled over and saw her. She was in the hammock and she had that book in front of her face. But like she said, she didn't have any idea. Do you perhaps?"

The woman looked at her disdainfully.

"I'm not in the habit of giving directions to liquor stores to strange women in the middle of the afternoon. Don't you have a phone?"

"I do," Jessie said. "But I was having trouble getting a signal."

Out of the corner of her eye, she saw Hannah hold the book up to her face for real, obviously attempting to hide her silent laughter.

"You know, you look kind of familiar to me," the woman said.

"I get that a lot," Jessie said nervously before trying to play it off. "People say I remind them of someone not-quite-famous."

The woman didn't smile.

"Please get off my porch," she said firmly.

"Of course," Jessie obliged. "Sorry for the confusion."

She turned and started back down the steps.

"Have a nice day," Hannah yelled after her.

"You too, young lady," Jessie said politely as she hurried back down the walk to the car and yelled out to Ryan. "They don't know, honey!"

When she got in the car, he did her the courtesy of waiting until she'd pulled out before speaking.

"What the hell was all that about?"

She just shook her head, her mind swimming with too many thoughts to offer a coherent response.

I have a sister. And she's a piece of work.

CHAPTER TWENTY SIX

Jessie was not ready.

In order for the re-interview with the Horsleys to prove useful, she needed to be focused and prepared to pick up on any nonverbal cues they might give. But her head was not in it. Flashes of what had just happened kept forcing their way into her mind. Waves of emotion were crashing just below the surface—concern, suspicion and a deep longing to connect more deeply with the troubled half-sister she had been unaware of until recently.

But there wasn't time for any of that. They took the hospital elevator up to Cal Horsley's office and had just stepped out into the hall when Ryan turned to her.

"Are you sure you're up for this?" he asked. "You still seem shaken up by that thing with the Dorsey girl."

"Yeah—I'll be okay," she assured him with more confidence than she felt. "You know I'm a pressure player. As soon as we're in there, I'll have my game face on."

"So now you're using sports metaphors?" he said skeptically, though he was smiling. "Now I *know* something's off with you."

"Hey," she protested, embracing his attempt at humor, "just because I'm not a huge sports fan doesn't mean I don't understand the lingo. Now let's get in there and score a touchdown before the bottom of the ninth."

He didn't reply, merely shaking his head as he knocked on the door marked "Dr. Callum Horsley, Pediatric Cardiology." It was opened moments later, to their surprise, by Meadow Horsley. She smiled broadly and welcomed them in.

"I heard you were here. Cal just finished surgery and is washing up. He asked me to greet you and let you know he should be back any minute. Can I offer either of you anything in the interim—coffee, water?"

"I think we're good," Jessie said, trying to recalibrate their plan. The goal was to question Cal privately about his interactions with Taylor. But it looked like getting him away from Meadow without drawing her suspicion might be difficult.

"What's this all about?" Meadow asked, confirming Jessie's concern. "I was surprised that you didn't ask to speak to both of us."

"Oh, we just had some follow-ups for him and we didn't want to bother you unnecessarily," Ryan said, employing his best casual voice.

"It's no bother," Meadow assured them. Jessie noticed again how the woman seemed to be almost pulsating without moving, her coiled energy was so vibrant.

"Do you ever get sick of each other?' she asked suddenly, hoping to stall by changing the subject.

"What?" Meadow asked, perplexed.

"You and Cal—you live together, you work together, you commute together. I just wondered if it got old after a while."

"Is this just curiosity?" Meadow asked, glancing between Jessie and Ryan, "Or do you have a personal stake in the answer?"

"Just curious," Jessie answered more quickly than she was proud of. "It just seems like a lot."

Meadow smiled sneakily, aware that she'd hit a nerve, but said nothing about that.

"It's not as much time together as you might think, especially here. Cal is in surgery or checking on patients most of the day. I'm constantly in meetings or on the phone. We try to have lunch together if our schedules allow. But often, we'll go entire days at work without seeing each other."

Just then the door opened and Cal Horsley joined them. As Meadow stepped over to hug him, Ryan gave Jessie an approving nod. He must have liked her stalling technique.

"Sorry for the delay," Cal said. "I was just wrapping up a tricky procedure on a newborn with a leaking ventricle."

"Is the baby okay?" Jessie asked. She silently chastised herself for her inability to hide her concern.

"She's better than she was," he answered. "I suspect we'll have to go back in next week. But for now at least, she's stable. But enough about me—what can I do for you?'

Ryan and Jessie looked at each other, debating how to proceed. Ryan finally took the lead.

"Dr. Horsley . . ."

"Cal," Cal insisted.

"Cal," Ryan consented, "we have few questions for you that might be of a sensitive nature. Maybe you'd like to talk to us privately?"

The Horsleys looked at each with a shared expression of anxiety and defensiveness, after which Meadow raised her eyes at her husband challengingly. Jessie thought she heard the woman's teeth grinding.

"Anything you want to ask me," he finally said, "you can ask in front of my wife. I don't have any secrets from her. That's how we live our life."

Ryan shrugged and looked at Jessie, who suspected the guy was going to regret his choice. Still, she nodded at Ryan to let him know she thought he should proceed. He didn't waste time.

"When we interviewed you at your home, you said that you only watched when your wife and Taylor engaged in sexual activity. Is that still your representation?"

Cal shifted slightly on his feet and half-glanced at Meadow, who seemed to be as curious as they were about his response. After an unexpected coughing jag that seemed to come out of nowhere, Cal answered.

"That might not have been strictly accurate. You aren't like the FBI, are you, where lying to them is itself a crime?"

"You're well advised to be truthful with us, Dr. Horsley," Ryan said, dispensing with the "Cal" bit.

"Okay," Cal said slowly. "Then here's a more robust version of the truth. Initially, yes, I only watched and provided support when certain activities had an element of risk."

"Initially?" Jessie pressed. "What does that mean?"

"I'd say that lasted for about a month."

"And then what happened?" she asked.

Cal stood silently, either unwilling or unable to respond.

"Then," Meadow interjected," we invited him to join in."

"What?" Ryan said, shocked.

"You have to understand," Meadow continued. "This was the first time Taylor had ever done anything like this. It was all new to her. And while she was excited, it took a while to develop trust among us, for her to feel totally comfortable. When we felt like she was okay with where we were at, I privately broached the idea with her of including Cal. She was receptive. So he started joining us."

"Why lie about that?" Jessie demanded, not revealing that Taylor was actually more experienced with threesomes than Meadow seemed to know.

"Look," Cal said gently. "Some people can't handle what we're into. The looks on your faces when we explained BDSM suggested you were among them. I'd like to think I'm evolved enough to not be bothered by that kind of reaction. But the truth is—I felt judged by you. And I figured that telling you that I did more than watch would lead to even more judgment. So I copped out. I'm not proud of it. And I'm sorry I wasn't honest."

Jessie glanced over at Ryan, who looked noncommittal. She wasn't entirely convinced herself. Cal Horsley didn't seem like the type to embarrass easily. She wondered if the real reason he hadn't been honest was because he knew about the pregnancy and didn't want them to ask the question she was about to.

"Would you be willing to take a paternity test?" she asked directly.

Cal's eyes nearly popped out of his head.

"Was Taylor pregnant?" he asked, stunned.

"She was," Jessie said, not volunteering anything else.

"I... of course," he said quietly.

"Do you mind if we ask for a DNA sample now?" Jessie continued, hoping to take advantage of his vulnerable state. "We're on a tight timetable here."

"I'm happy to do it right away," he said with an unexpected hint of melancholy in his voice. "But is it possible to handle this discreetly? I'd rather not ask the lab here. It might get out."

"We'll have a medical tech come here and get the sample," Ryan told him. "They can do the test on site anonymously. No one will know it's you."

Cal seemed hesitant, then decided against objecting.

"So after all these years of helping children," he said wistfully, "I only find out that I might have had one of my own on the way after it's passed on."

Jessie didn't know how to respond to that and looked away. She happened to catch a glimpse of Meadow Horsley, who had tears in her eyes. It was not the reaction that Jessie would have expected and she was thoroughly flummoxed by it.

She had no idea whether she was dealing with a murder, a suicide or a tragic accident. For the first time since she'd seen Taylor Jansen lying dead in her bed, Jessie was completely at a loss.

Jessie couldn't drink another sip.

She was on her third cup of crappy coffee from the hospital cafeteria and each one seemed worse than the last.

She and Ryan had decided that with Decker's "end of the day" ultimatum, they were better off just waiting at the hospital for Cal Horsley's paternity results rather than going back to the station. So they were stuck in the cafeteria, reviewing the additional reports that had come in from the tech unit.

Unfortunately, nothing in them seemed helpful. According to the person who'd done the follow-up review of Gavin Peck's laptop location data, he either really was home working on Monday or he was a brilliant computer genius hiding in plain sight, one who had flawlessly spoofed his own location to make it look like he'd never left home.

If that was the case, Jessie doubted he'd spend his professional hours designing personal websites for bodybuilders and power lifters. It would be a waste of his formidable skills. His motive might be the most compelling of any suspect, but if they couldn't find any way to tie him to Taylor's apartment, it was moot.

Claire Shine's alibi remained solid. There were multiple Facebook photos from her supplement soirees, most time-stamped. If she had done this, it must have been through a proxy because her time was fully accounted for.

Jessie wondered if maybe *she* could have secured a hired gun from the Propov crime family. They'd been so fixated on whether Doug might have paid someone to take Taylor out that they hadn't considered if Claire might be capable of that. Jessie continued to believe that she was really the planner in the family. Doug seemed to be coasting along on sleazy charm and a disregard for ethics. Claire was more of a hustler.

But according to Reggie Toney in Organized Crime, nothing about what happened in Taylor's apartment comported with how these assassins operated In fact, he didn't think any of them could pull it off.

"If this was a murder," he'd said on the phone after reviewing the file and photos, "it was way too sophisticated for anyone in the Propov crew. They aren't the type to delicately mask a murder as an accident or possible suicide. You'd know it was them, even if they didn't want you to."

With that disappointing assessment still lingering, Jessie reconsidered the Horsleys. Their alibis were still holding up. And neither seemed to have a compelling motive. Meadow looked like a woman who would happily be carrying on with Taylor at this very moment if she could.

Cal had admittedly been cagey, but he'd come clean when asked if he'd ever slept with Taylor and volunteered to take the paternity test without an argument. He even seemed a little upset that he had come close to potentially being a father and not known it. If that reaction was genuine, then it undermined his clearest motive to kill the mother, even if it wasn't his wife.

Just as she was turning those thoughts over in her head, Ryan got a call. He answered it, listened intently for a few seconds, thanked the caller and hung up.

"Good news?" Jessie asked.

"I honestly have no idea," he replied.

"Well, don't keep me in suspense."

"The paternity test came back. Cal Horsley was the father of Taylor Jansen's unborn child."

Jessie sat with the news for a second. She didn't know what to make of it either.

"Well," she finally suggested. "Let's confront him with it—see how he reacts."

"What's the point, Jessie? He won't be shocked by the news. He seemed to be halfway hoping it was true. The fact that he's the father doesn't seem to make him any more or less of a suspect."

Jessie, without any way to counter him, instead took another sip from the liquid monstrosity in the Styrofoam cup, then spit it out, unable to swallow any more.

"I wonder how often they change the coffee filters here," she muttered irritably "Maybe every few months?"

"Don't take your frustration out on the fine cafeteria staff here, Ms. Hunt," Ryan gently chastised her. "I'm sure they switch them out every few weeks."

Jessie looked at him as a thought began to form in her head.

"What?" he said, confused by her sudden focus. "You started it. Don't act like I'm the gross-out guy here."

"No," she muttered, waving him off as she opened up the case file looking for the relevant page.

"Here it is," she finally said, grabbing the sheet she'd been looking for.

"What's that?"

"When you said they probably change the filters every few weeks, it occurred to me that the difference between a few weeks can be a very big deal."

"I'm not following," he admitted.

"What I'm saying, Detective Hernandez, is that I am holding proof that Dr. Callum Horsley is a straight-up liar."

CHAPTER TWENTY SEVEN

At the tables nearby, all conversation stopped. Jessie glanced over and saw several nurses at one table staring at her in open-mouthed silence. At another, two orderlies picked up their trays and hurried off as quickly as they could without actually running.

"Care to tell me what the hell you're talking about?" Ryan hissed.

"The math doesn't add up," she replied. "They supposedly began their fling with Taylor two months ago. But Cal only became an active participant one month ago?"

"Okay."

"Look at the medical examiner's preliminary report. It says Taylor was about seven weeks pregnant. For that to be possible, even allowing for some margin of error, this means Cal was involved with Taylor before he claimed to be, probably very soon after they started this whole arrangement."

Ryan nodded, now on board.

"So he lied about when he first had sex with Taylor," he said. "The question is: why? Was he trying to hide his involvement with Taylor from his wife or just from us?"

"If Meadow knew already, I don't see any reason he wouldn't be forthcoming with us at that point."

"Maybe so we wouldn't suspect him of being the father," he suggested.

"That doesn't make sense. First, he claims he didn't know she was pregnant. And even if he did, he's a physician. He had to know that the pregnancy would be discovered at some point and we'd find out that he lied. Unless I'm missing something, the only logical reason to do that is to keep his wife from knowing."

"And if he was trying to keep it from her," Ryan added, starting to warm up to the theory, "that gives him a motive to keep Taylor quiet. Maybe she wanted to come clean. Maybe she was blackmailing him."

"Right," Jessie agreed. "And as a doctor working in a hospital, he'd have fairly easy access to medication like sleeping pills. I'm sure he could get past whatever security precautions the hospital takes in order to secure what he needed and no one would ever know."

"Of course," Ryan noted, "all that is just circumstantial. His alibi is still rock solid. So, I say we go back at him, threaten to reveal the truth to Meadow unless he comes clean."

"Actually, I had a different idea," Jessie countered. "I say we put them together. I want to see how his devoted wife reacts when we challenge him."

"Why?"

"Because I have my doubts about just how devoted she is," Jessie said. "Haven't you noticed that there seems to be some tension underneath the whole 'completely open, nonjudgmental' vibe they put out?"

"I actually hadn't," he admitted.

"Typical male," Jessie teased. "Even when he's a professional police detective, he can't pick up the signs."

Ryan was quiet for a second.

"Apparently not," he said resignedly.

Jessie realized too late that her comment need not only apply to the Horsleys but to his own failing marriage.

"Oh, hey . . . I didn't mean."

"That's okay," he interrupted, sounding rueful. "I probably deserved that, even if you didn't mean it that way. Don't worry about it, Jessie. Let's deal with this messed up marriage before deconstructing mine."

"Fair enough," she agreed, deciding to let it lie though she felt the strong urge not to.

They met with the Horsleys in an administrative conference room this time. Jessie didn't want Cal to have the home court advantage of his office. She wanted him as uncomfortable as he could be without actually taking him down to the station.

As everyone settled in to the cushy, high-backed chairs, Jessie studied the couple closely. Meadow still had a big smile and that high-wire energy, even though it was late afternoon. Cal looked less excited and perhaps a little nervous.

Ryan intentionally exacerbated that feeling by standing back up as soon as everyone else was seated. He walked over and lowered the blinds by the window, making the sterile, unwelcoming environment even more so.

"You get the results?" Cal asked with a mix of sadness and trepidation.

"We did," Ryan told him. "You *were* the father."

Cal looked over at Meadow, then at Jessie.

"It's hard to even know how to feel about this. How do I mourn something I didn't even know existed until today? I have this strange pit in my stomach but I don't really understand why."

"Maybe it's for another reason, Dr. Horsley," Ryan suggested.

"Cal," he corrected. "What do you mean?"

"Dr. Horsley," Ryan continued, pointedly rejecting Cal's suggestion this time. "It turns out that at the time of her death, Taylor Jansen was approximately seven weeks pregnant. And we know that you're the father. But you said you only began sleeping with her a month ago. How do you explain that?"

There was a long pause, during which Cal looked from Ryan to Meadow, who was staring at him open-mouthed, and back again.

"Well," he eventually rasped, "clearly that timeline reflects poorly on me."

Under other circumstances, Jessie would have laughed at his audacity, but not now.

"I agree," she said slowly. "Maybe you can clear that up for us."

"Obviously," he started to say, looking at the table in front of him rather than in anyone's eyes, "Taylor and I had sex earlier than I previously indicated. I didn't want to say anything because I didn't want to hurt Meadow and frankly, I didn't think it mattered that much."

Out of the corner of her eye, Jessie saw Meadow Horsley visibly flinch at that last comment. Hoping to keep the questioning focused, she jumped right back in.

"How and when did it begin?" Jessie asked.

Cal gave his wife a furtive glance before returning his attention to the tabletop.

"Taylor came on to me privately soon after she and Meadow first hooked up. She said she was turned on by me watching but that it wasn't enough for her. She wanted to consummate things. I told her that would be a violation of the rules. But she was very persuasive. In the end, much to my shame, I gave in."

"When was the first time?" Jessie pressed.

"Within days of the first time she was with Meadow, maybe after their second encounter."

"Where?" Ryan asked.

"Usually at the house, when I knew Meadow would be out. On rare occasions at her place. But none of that has anything to do with her death, I swear. It was just a romp, nothing more. Yes, I cheated. But I didn't kill her!"

Apparently that was the final straw for Meadow.

"How do we know that?" she screamed. "How do we know anything you say is true?"

Cal looked at her, shocked at her outburst. He quickly tried to recover.

"Meadow, you can't possibly believe I would do this? What reason could I have?"

"To hide your affair from me!" she shot back. "To hide the pregnancy."

"I didn't even know she was pregnant," he protested.

"You say that now," she chided. "But until these people called you on it, you were happy to hide your deception."

"It meant nothing, Meadow. I was just scratching an itch."

Meadow shook her head in disgust.

"We're supposed to scratch those itches together," she entreated him. "If you had come to me, do you think I would have objected? The whole point of this is to be open and honest. But you weren't. You never are."

"What does that mean?" he demanded, the apologetic tone fading away.

Jessie wondered the same thing.

"You know what it means," Meadow seethed, her teeth bared and her eyes glinting with rage. "You act a good game, Callum 'call me Cal' Horsley. But we both know you're a narcissistic fame whore. And I'm just your glorified PR flunky."

Cal stared at her, seemingly stunned, for several seconds before finally replying.

"And what about you?" he asked slowly, his tone switching from righteous indignation to a kind of quiet fuming. "As long as we're being open and forthcoming, shall we share with the fine investigators how you are so frigid and sexless that the only way I can get you to sleep with me is to bring another woman along for the ride?"

Meadow barely waited for him to finish before firing back.

"The world is probably better off with you having less sex, Callum. For a guy whose professional mission is to save kids, you would have made a terrible parent—selfish, short-tempered and devoid of empathy."

"Ditto, dear. I doubt you could raise a Betta fish, much less a human child."

They both stopped yelling and stared silently at each other with such venom that Jessie thought one of them might actually spit at the other. She stayed quiet, as did Ryan, hoping that these outbursts might lead to some kind of revelation that could undermine an alibi or give a clearer motive. But they seemed to have shouted themselves out.

"Maybe we should continue this conversation down at the station, Dr. Horsley," Ryan suggested.

"Are you arresting me?" the man snapped before regaining some control. "I'm sorry for my tone."

"We're not arresting you," Ryan said, ignoring the apology. "But we do have more questions. And your cooperation would go a long way toward eliminating you as a suspect. Are you willing to answer those questions?"

"I'm willing to go with you, just to get away from *her*," he said sharply, nodding disdainfully at Meadow. "But I don't know that I have any more answers for you."

"Well, we'll work that out together," Ryan said, indicating for the doctor to stand up.

Jessie looked at him, trying to convey her confusion with a hard stare. He mouthed "wait" to her and turned his attention to Meadow Horsley.

"Why don't you go home?" he suggested. "Someone will check in with you a little later, okay?"

Meadow nodded, though she didn't really seem to be paying attention to his words. When they got out in the hall, Jessie waited until Cal was out of earshot before whispering to Ryan.

"Why aren't you arresting him?" she demanded.

"For what, lying?" he asked.

"Suspicion of murder," Jessie countered.

"We don't have enough to arrest him on anything yet, Jessie. He's definitely shady and maybe far worse than that. But lying about infidelity isn't a crime in itself. Yeah, maybe he has more of a motive now than before. But it's not clear cut. As we just saw in there, he wasn't lying to save his perfect marriage. It sounds like that was teetering anyway. Besides, we still haven't found any way to puncture his alibi. Unless that happens, this is all just speculation."

"So, what, he's just going to get away with this?" she asked incredulously.

"First of all," he said, "we still don't know that there's anything to get away with. I continue to have doubts that this is even a murder. Second, if he did do this, then let's find out. He's coming back to the station. I'll Mirandize him and then we'll turn the screws on him and see what happens. Maybe he'll crack. We need to take advantage of his willingness to talk while we can. Once he lawyers up, we're out of luck."

"I'm starting to worry that we're already out of luck," Jessie muttered.

"Hey, don't be such a Debbie Downer," he said flashing the smile that reminded her why she was drawn to him in the first place.

Despite her misgivings, she couldn't help but grin back.

CHAPTER TWENTY EIGHT

The grin disappeared quickly.

Back at the station interrogation room, Cal Horsley had mostly clammed up. Every time Ryan got aggressive in his questioning, Cal mused on whether he should call his lawyer. Gone was the deferential, sophisticated healer. In his place was the very man Meadow had described—narcissistic and seemingly without empathy for his wife or even Taylor. Strangely, his new persona worked to his advantage.

By not hiding what a self-involved jerk he was, he seemed to be revealing how confident he was that they wouldn't find out anything worse about him. He didn't actually say it but his bearing seemed to announce, "Yeah, I'm an asshole. But that's not a crime, so screw off."

After a long impasse, Jessie tried a different tack.

"I don't get it. If your marriage was basically over, why did you even care if Meadow found out about the affair? Better yet, why not just divorce her so you could have your fun out in the open?"

"Are you kidding?" he asked as if she was in idiot. "Why would I do that when I had the best of both worlds? Meadow is the perfect show horse wife. Like she said, she's basically my unpaid publicist. She looks good on my arm. She rakes in a ton of money for the hospital, which reflects well on me. And after some clever manipulation, I got her to agree to let me screw her personal trainer, who she was besotted with. And what a trainer she was. Let me tell you, Meadow may have been the show horse, but Taylor was a real work horse, if you know what I mean."

Jessie felt a bit of bile churn in her stomach and fought the urge to throw up. Instead, she swallowed hard, smiled, and continued, trying another approach.

"You said Meadow was infatuated with Taylor. Do you think that maybe she secretly found out about your affair? Is there any chance ...".

He cut her off.

"Don't try to pin this on Meadow," he chided. "Look, she may be a low-grade bitch but that doesn't mean I'm going to accuse her of killing someone. She never would have harmed her one true love. Besides, I was with her with pretty much every second she wasn't working on Monday. I'd have noticed if she had gone missing for an extended stretch."

Just then, there was a knock on the door and the always-enthusiastic rookie Officer Beatty poked his head in. His blond hair looked windblown and his uniform hung loosely on his gangly body.

"May I have a word?" he asked, his voice calm though his eyes were less so.

Jessie nodded and she and Ryan stood up. As they walked to the door, he leaned in and muttered in her ear.

"Good idea, trying to get him to throw Meadow under the bus. If we can get them to turn on each other in a real way, maybe we can break this thing open."

When they stepped outside, Jessie could tell that something was really bothering Officer Beatty.

"What's wrong?" she asked.

"There's a man named Gavin Peck in the station lobby. He's waving a gun around and saying he wants justice. He says the only person he'll talk to is you."

Jessie looked at Ryan, who appeared as stunned as she felt. Without a word, they both sprinted in the direction of the lobby. It took a good forty-five seconds, leaving Jessie bent over and winded when they arrived. Ryan looked like he was struggling too. When they were just outside the lobby door, they peeked through the small window.

Gavin Peck was indeed standing in the middle of the lobby, alternately holding a gun to his head and pointing it at anyone who even flinched.

"You talk to him," Ryan said between gasps of air, "I'll stand next to you, armed. If I say duck, you duck, got it?"

She nodded, trying to catch her breath. They were about to step through the door when Officer Beatty came tearing around the corner, almost running into them. He was holding two bulletproof vests.

"Thanks," Jessie said, as they strapped them on. Once that was done, Ryan grabbed the door and Jessie called out.

"Gavin, it's Jessie Hunt. I heard you want to talk to me. I'm coming through the door on your left, okay?"

Gavin turned in her direction.

"No tricks!" he shouted.

"No tricks," she repeated. "I'm coming out now. Detective Hernandez is with me. He is armed. But he promises not to get into any wrestling matches with you, okay?"

Gavin didn't smile but he didn't object either. Jessie took it as a positive sign and nodded for Ryan to open the door. He did and she stepped through into the lobby.

What was clear now that she hadn't been able to discern from peeking through the small window was just how many people were in the room. In addition to the three officers behind the main desk, there were easily fifteen civilians in the waiting area. Most were crouched behind chairs or hiding in corners.

Gavin was standing in the middle of the room, holding a handgun. When Jessie entered, he pointed it first at her, then at his own head. He was sweating profusely and his eyes were wild. He wore a sweatshirt and tight bike shorts. On his feet were flips-flops.

"What's going on, Gavin?" she asked, both trying to engage him and understand the truly perplexing sight in front of her.

"I know what happened!" he shouted. "I know who did it!"

"Who did what?" she inquired, keeping her tone level.

"Who killed Taylor!"

"Okay," Jessie soothed. "Who did, Gavin?"

"It was Horsley, the doctor," he said with frenzied conviction.

Jessie was taken aback. She didn't think Gavin even knew who Cal Horsley was.

"What makes you say that?" she asked evenly, giving away nothing.

"I heard it," he insisted as he waved his gun in her direction. "I heard you two talking about it."

She looked over at Ryan, who seemed to be at a loss too. But he also looked like he wasn't in the mood to play twenty questions. His finger rested gently on the trigger of his weapon.

"Okay," Jessie said, trying to put that out of her head. "I'm happy to discuss all of this with you, Gavin. But first, I need you to stop waving that gun all around. It's making my colleagues nervous. More importantly, how can we have a thoughtful discussion of your allegation under this kind of stress? We need to tamp everything down. I want to hear you out. But it's hard when I'm worried you're going to shoot me. Can you help lower the temperature in here by lowering the gun?"

As she said it, it really seemed to Jessie like the actual temperature had been jacked up in the lobby. She felt drops of cold perspiration magically appear under her arms and roll down her side. Despite that, she raised her arms above her head and took a slow but definitive step toward him.

"If I drop the gun, I don't have any leverage," Gavin protested.

"Leverage for what?" Jessie asked. "You don't need to hold a gun for us to investigate your charges. So what do you have it for?"

"Someone needs to make him pay and it doesn't sound like you're going to."

"What do you mean, Gavin?" Jessie asked, genuinely mystified at how he knew so much.

Gavin hesitated briefly, as if he knew what he was about to say might not be kosher.

"Gavin," she persisted, "you're already holding a gun in a police station. You're not going to get in worse trouble by spilling what you know."

That seemed to resonate with him.

"I put a bug on him," he said, nodding at Ryan. "When we got in our tussle, I stuck it to his shirt. Later on, when I got home, I played back my recording of what he'd said. It cut in and out a lot and eventually stopped working altogether. But I got enough to know that Horsley was a suspect. So I tapped into the station's communication system to listen in to all the police traffic. I heard someone say you were bringing him in for questioning and I knew what that meant. So I came over."

"But why the gun, Gavin?"

"He's a big-time doctor with lots of powerful connections. And from what I heard, you guys weren't going to be able to nail him. So I thought maybe..."

"Maybe you'd deliver some justice of your own?" Jessie asked leadingly.

Gavin seemed temporarily less sure of himself before regaining a bit of the intensity in his eyes.

"Someone has to!"

"Gavin," she said softly, now standing only feet away from him, "this guy may be guilty. But we don't know that yet. It's also entirely possible that he's just an unbelievable narcissist who doesn't truly care about anything other than satisfying his own basest needs. Either way, you trying to deliver some kind of vigilante justice won't help Taylor. Let us do our job. If he's guilty, we'll find out and he'll go down. Don't ruin your future over this guy. It's not worth it."

Gavin looked at her helplessly, the intensity leaving his eyes. Then he leaned in and whispered to her.

"The gun's not loaded. I forgot to bring bullets."

Jessie suddenly felt as if an anvil had been ripped off her chest. Though she couldn't be certain he was telling the truth, his body language suggested he was.

"That's actually a good thing," she whispered back. "It shows you didn't really have deadly intentions. It'll make it easier to argue for leniency with the D.A. But to really make that case, you need to hand me the gun. And then you need to follow all the orders you're given, okay?"

Gavin nodded, though he made no move.

"We can salvage this, Gavin," she said gently. "If you make the right moves from here on in. Are you ready?"

He nodded again.

"Okay," Jessie said so that everyone in the room can hear, "Mr. Peck is going to hand over the weapon now. He has agreed to comply with all instructions."

She looked back at Gavin, who carefully placed his gun in her outstretched hands. The second he'd done so, Ryan began to speak.

"Jessie, take three steps back," he instructed, his weapon still trained on Peck. "Gavin, please get on your knees and place your hands in the air above you. An officer is going to come over and handcuff you. Do not resist. Do you understand? I need a verbal confirmation."

"I understand," Gavin said clearly, doing as he was instructed.

As he was being cuffed, Jessie leaned in and spoke to him quietly.

"Gavin, I understand your frustration. And we're doing everything we can for Taylor. But you need to think about your own future right now. Do everything that is asked of you. Comply willingly. Don't be combative. I'm going to try to get them to go easier on you. But I can't do any of that unless you are a model of good behavior from now on. We clear?'

"We're clear," he said in a defeated voice.

The officer who cuffed him instructed him to get to his feet and led him out of the lobby. As they left, Jessie couldn't help but wonder if anything she'd just said held any weight. Could she really do anything to help Gavin? And in the back of her mind, another question lingered:

Should I?

Someone who managed to bug Ryan in the middle of a fight and access the police communications system was almost certainly capable of manipulating location data. Gavin Peck seemed like a lovesick guy out to avenge his former lover's murder. But what if that was exactly the image he wanted to project?

Jessie barely had time to breathe.

Just as Gavin was being escorted off to booking, Officer Beatty, who'd given them the vests, approached her and Ryan. He looked hesitant to speak.

"Go ahead," Ryan said. "Whatever you've got for us, it's clearly bad news. May as well just pile on at this point."

"I'm sorry, Detective," Beatty said. "But Callum Horsley is making a fuss in the interrogation room. He says that unless you all return immediately, he's leaving or asking for a lawyer."

Ryan and Jessie looked at each other, both exhausted.

"Maybe we should have waited a few more weeks before coming back to work," Ryan said with a wry smile.

"A little late for that," Jessie noted. "We better get back there."

"Hold up," Ryan said, the turned to the officer. "Tell him we had a momentary crisis and that we'll be back in two minutes."

The officer nodded and rushed off.

"We better not mess around with this guy," Jessie warned. "Why the delay?"

"Let me ask you, do you think we can now officially rule Gavin Peck out as a suspect?"

Jessie looked at him, perplexed by the question.

Probably," she finally conceded. "I mean, it did occur to me that he staged this elaborate scenario to throw suspicion off himself, even at the risk of being charged with a lesser crime. But that would require a level of cunning I'm not sure he's capable of. Why?"

"Because I agree with you," Ryan said. "I think that if this was a murder, it was committed by someone extremely cunning, someone who is so confident in his skills that he's willing to answer police questions without a lawyer, look like a complete scumbag and make demands that detectives be at his beck and call, all because he's sure he's untouchable. The person who fits that description isn't Gavin. It's Cal Horsley."

"Okay," Jessie conceded. "So what's your point?"

"So let's make him touchable," Ryan said. "I still think the best way to do that is through his wife. If we can get her to flip on him, maybe we've got a shot. Maybe she was covering for his alibi even if she wasn't with him every second. If so, perhaps she's having second thoughts about that decision. I don't think we'll get a better shot at turning her."

"So what do you propose?" Jessie asked.

"You go talk to her. Bond with her over cheating, murderous husbands. Convince her that her fate isn't tied to his. Meanwhile, I'll keep Cal occupied, let him run me around in circles. Maybe he'll let something slip. Even if he doesn't, it'll give you time to wear Meadow down. What do you think?"

"I think that anything that keeps me out of the same room as that skin-crawling slimeball is worth a shot."

"Then go," he insisted. "Just keep me apprised. I'll stay with the skin crawler."

"With that name, you make him sound like some kind of comic book super villain," she said.

"I'm starting to wonder," he replied.

CHAPTER TWENTY NINE

Jessie moved quickly.

She wasn't sure how long Ryan could keep Cal busy and she didn't want to risk him getting out of the station and putting pressure on Meadow. As she approached the couple's Los Feliz mansion she got a call. It was from Reggie Toney in Organized Crime.

"Hey, Hunt, I know you're not formally a detective but I was told Hernandez is conducting an interrogation and thought one of you should hear the info I just got."

"What's that?" she asked as she pulled into the Horsley driveway.

"Claire Shine was found shot to death earlier this afternoon in her home."

Jessie hit the brakes hard, causing the wheels to screech.

"What?" she asked, dumbfounded. "What about Doug?"

"He's nowhere to be found," Reggie said. "His car is missing and no one has seen him since his last meeting around 2 p.m. We've got an APB out on his vehicle and have even sent Border Patrol a description in case he's headed for Mexico."

The front door of the Horsley house opened to reveal Meadow, looking confused. Jessie rolled down her window.

"I'll be right with you," she called out before returning to the phone. "Do you think this is related to our case?"

"No way to know yet," Reggie admitted. "It could be. From what you told us, it sounded like their pending divorce was already pretty acrimonious. Maybe being investigated for murder made him snap. Then again, it could have something to do with the Propovs. It's just too early to know. Regardless, I wanted to warn you that he's out there somewhere, probably not happy with you and potentially armed and dangerous. You should stay alert."

"Thanks, Reggie," she said. She hung up but continued to pretend she was on the phone, hoping to use the extra time to formulate a game plan.

Part of her wanted to just turn around and go back to the comparative security of the station. If Doug Shine was driving around the city, possibly looking for payback, she was probably near the top of his list. But if Claire's death was unrelated to their investigation, then talking to Meadow and convincing her to tell her about anything suspicious Cal had done was essential.

There was really only one move. She couldn't do anything about Doug Shine right now. But Meadow Horsley was standing right in front of her. That had to be her focus.

"Sorry about that," she said as she got out of the car. "Another case reared its head. They like to keep us busy."

"I understand," Meadow said, still looking apprehensive. "But I'm surprised to see you without Cal. I assumed you were here to drop him off."

"No, he's still down at the station, talking to Detective Hernandez. I was hoping you and I could chat for a few minutes."

"Sure, I guess," she agreed, her normal bubbliness understandably subdued. "Please come in."

They returned to the same living room where they'd spoken the first time, passing the hallway bathroom that Jessie had pretended to use.

"Can I get you something?" Meadow asked. "Water? Tea? Coffee? Something stronger maybe? I've already dipped into a few glasses of Sauvignon Blanc."

"Some hot tea would be great, thanks," Jessie said. She wasn't really that interested but figured that leaning into the niceties of the situation might get Meadow to loosen up and be more forthcoming.

"I should probably switch over to that too," Meadow asked as she stepped into the adjacent kitchen to put on the kettle. "When will Cal be coming back?"

Jessie was a bit surprised by the question.

"What makes you think he's coming back at all, Meadow?" she replied. "He's under investigation in Taylor's death. You yourself sounded like you thought he might be guilty back in that conference room."

"I was just upset," Meadow said, stepping back into the living room while the water boiled. "I had just found out my husband had been cheating on me with the woman we were supposed to be sharing. I guess I lashed out."

"I'm not sure I would l call it lashing out so much as righteous anger," Jessie countered. "I know a little something about this sort of thing."

"I doubt it," Meadow said dismissively.

"You might be surprised. A couple of years ago I was in a very different situation than I am now. I was married to a wealthy businessman, living in a big house like this. I thought my life was going pretty well. Within a matter of months I discovered that my husband had been having an affair, that he killed his mistress when she threatened to tell me and that he was trying to frame me for her murder. He even poisoned me at one point when I was pregnant, leading to a miscarriage. That was before he stabbed me with a fireplace poker."

Meadow's mouth dropped open.

"Are you for real?" she asked.

"I am. All that really happened. But for a long time, even when the signs were staring me in the face, I refused to accept that my husband wasn't the man I thought he was. And my job is to profile people for a living."

Meadow was quiet for several seconds, looking at her carpet. When she finally looked back up, there were tears in her eyes.

"So, what are you saying?" she asked helplessly.

"I'm saying that maybe it's time to ask some hard questions about your husband. You've described him as narcissistic and without empathy. Could he be more than that? You're his alibi for that morning and evening. Are you sure you want to stand by that? In general, no one would blame you for trying to protect your husband. But if you're protecting him when he might have killed someone, that's a different matter altogether. If you do that, you become culpable too."

The water began to boil and Meadow returned to the kitchen. Jessie sat on the couch quietly, wondering if she'd made any impact. If Meadow was covering for her husband, this might be their last chance to get her to admit it. Once Cal left that interrogation room, the lawyers would likely take over and pressure her to keep her mouth shut.

A minute later, Meadow returned to the living room with a tray comprised of a teapot, two cups on fancy saucers and a plate filled with biscotti. She poured Jessie a cup and then one for herself. Jessie grabbed a sugar, trying to act unconcerned as she mixed it into her tea.

She could sense that this was the moment of truth. Either Meadow would share what she really knew and they had a shot at taking down Cal or fear would keep her in check and she'd shut down. After a good thirty seconds of sugar-mixing, she couldn't pretend any longer. She took a sip and looked up at the woman across from her.

She knew immediately that Meadow wasn't going to spill.

The woman had an expression somewhere between shame and defiance. Jessie waited for her to speak.

"Ms. Hunt, as much as I'd like to help you, as much as I'd love to bury that cheating hypocrite, I just can't. The timetable I gave you for Monday was accurate. I'm not covering for Cal. We drove to work together, worked all day and drove home that night. Now, can I vouch for every second of his time in the hospital? No. But he had multiple surgeries that no one else was capable of performing. So I don't see how, in the middle of all that, he found time to sneak out and kill Taylor. And truth be told, I just don't think he's capable of that."

"You'd be surprised," Jessie muttered.

"I'm sure I would," Meadow agreed. "And I know you've seen a lot more of the darkness in people than I have. But please don't project your personal experience onto my life. Just because your husband was capable of killing people doesn't mean mine is. He may be—hell, he *is* an asshole. But that doesn't diminish the fact that he saves lives, he doesn't take them. I could whip up some story for you. But it wouldn't be true. And then Taylor's killer would go free. I know you don't want that any more than I do."

Jessie nodded silently.

"No," she finally said. "I don't want that."

"I wish I could be more help," Meadow said remorsefully. "But I'm still trying to live by the mantra of my marriage even if Cal isn't."

"What was that again?" Jessie asked, though she was only half listening now. There wasn't much reason to continue the conversation at this point.

"We don't have any secrets. That's how we live our life."

"Right," Jessie recalled. "That's a good one, assuming both people are on board."

"That's the key," Meadow agreed.

"Well," Jessie said, standing up. "I hope that works out for you. I have to get back."

"Of course," Meadow said, standing up as well. "Do you think Cal will be coming home soon?"

"I expect that he will," Jessie said, unable to hide the disappointment in her voice. "I'll see myself out."

As she walked back down the long hallway to the front door, Jessie couldn't recall the last time she'd felt so defeated. Either Meadow Horsley was too blind to see the truth or too scared to share it. Either way, it looked like the bad guy was going to get away with it.

Jessie felt like crying.

Not so much because the likely killer of Taylor Jansen was going to get away scot-free. She had developed enough psychic calluses in her life to know that justice didn't always win out. But because she opened herself up emotionally as a means of catching him and it had failed.

She didn't like to talk about how she'd been played by her ex-husband. And she almost never mentioned the unborn child she'd lost at his hands. But she'd shared both of those painful horrors with Meadow in the hopes of connecting, all for naught. Meadow wasn't interested in connecting. She'd chosen her picture-perfect life over the truth and there was nothing Jessie could do about it.

Soon the Horsleys would be back to their old routine, going to cocktail party fundraisers, getting couple's massages and sharing their bed with willing young women they could enjoy guilt-free. They'd have secrets, but not from each other.

Not from each other.

Something about the phrase stuck in Jessie's mind, like a piece of gum stuck under a table that she couldn't scrape off.

"We don't have any secrets," Meadow had said. "That's how we live our life."

As Jessie sat in her car in the Horsley driveway, a provocative question bubbled to the surface of her jitterbugging brain.

What if that isn't just a cliché mantra? What if it's really the truth?

Chapter Thirty

Jessie made a phone call. And then another. And a third after that.

Over the next fifteen minutes, she made half a dozen calls, each with an increasing sense of tension, anticipation and what could only be described as hope. When she was done and got back out of the car, never having left the Horsley driveway, it was with a sense of purpose that she hadn't thought possible only minutes earlier.

She knocked on the door. As she waited, she looked around, wondering where Doug Shine might be right now. She doubted that he was nearby but stayed alert anyway. When Meadow opened the door this time, she looked more annoyed than anything.

"I'm sorry," Jessie said. "I was on an important call in my car and now I need to go to the bathroom. I don't think I'll make it back to the station. Could I borrow yours really quick?"

Meadow looked like she was tempted to refuse but ultimately opened the door and waved her in.

"Please be quick. I was just about to call the station to check on when I could go get Cal,"

"Of course," Jessie said reassuringly as she stepped inside and hurried down the hall. "I'll just be a minute."

Once in the bathroom, she configured herself, making sure everything was in order. When she felt confident that she was ready, she stepped back out. She could hear Meadow in the kitchen and headed that way. When she reached the massive room, she tried not to lose focus.

The Horsley kitchen was almost as big as Jessie's whole apartment, with a center island the size of a small car, two refrigerators and two double ovens. Meadow was at the double sink, washing dishes.

"You don't have someone to do that for you?" Jessie asked loudly over the sound of the water.

"We don't actually have a maid," Meadow replied, sounding mildly offended. "Besides, I find it relaxing. Is there anything else you need or shall I see you out now?"

"Actually, do you think I could get a top off on that tea before I go?"

Meadow looked at her in disbelief.

"First you try to get me to say my husband is a murderer and now you ask for more tea?"

"It wasn't personal, Meadow," Jessie said calmly, almost baitingly. "I'm just trying to get justice for Taylor. Should that prevent me from staying hydrated?"

Meadow said nothing but shook her head as she refilled the kettle.

"As long as we're waiting," Jessie continued. "I wanted to run something by you and see what you think."

"What's that?"

"It seems kind of weird that Cal's job is to interact with little kids all day and ultimately save their lives and yet he seems like he'd be a terrible parent."

"Why do you say that?" Meadow asked carefully.

"Actually you said it," Jessie reminded her. "Back in the conference room you called him selfish, short-tempered and devoid of empathy. That was right before he said he doubted you could raise a fish much less a child. In fact, neither of you seem to like kids that much."

"Just because we don't think we'd be great parents doesn't mean we don't like children," Meadow said defensively.

"You're probably right," Jessie agreed. "Forget I said it. You know what else is weird?"

"No. But I'm sure you'll tell me."

"Well, we had this one suspect in Taylor's death, her ex-boyfriend. But our problem was that his alibi seemed totally airtight. His digital footprint showed that he was home working on his laptop all day. But someone in our office suggested that maybe he could program his computer to operate remotely so that it looked like he was home even if he wasn't. Turns out that wasn't the case. I just spoke to one of our tech people who discovered that he was on several video calls and they show him in his house."

"So you're telling me you thought her ex was a suspect and now you don't?" Meadow said impatiently. "Why should I care about the dead ends of your case? Really, Ms. Hunt, I don't want to be rude but don't you think you've imposed on me enough for one day?"

"Absolutely," Jessie agreed. "And I'll head off right after I get that tea. But still, it got me thinking about how someone could make it seem like they were in one place when they were somewhere else. That's a pretty neat trick."

"I don't know," Meadow said. "Is it? I'm not a tech person."

"That's the wild thing," Jessie told her. "You don't have to be some tech genius to fake your location. I'm sure it helps. But if you plan carefully, you could still trick folks. Let's say, for example, and this is purely hypothetical, that when you and your husband were planning to drive home from the hospital on Monday night, at the last second he said he had to do one more thing in the office and sent you home ahead. And let's say he slipped his cell phone into the car without your knowledge."

The water began to boil. Meadow didn't go to it for a moment, letting the whistle grow louder, as she stared daggers at Jessie.

"You going to get that?" Jessie asked.

"I don't know. Are you going to keep throwing unfounded accusations at my husband?" Meadow shot back.

"Hey, I said it's just a hypothetical. I'm not making any accusations."

Meadow grunted and turned back to take the kettle off the burner. As she prepped the tea, she operatically kept her back to Jessie, refusing to even look at her.

"Anyway," Jessie continued, "in this hypothetical, Cal would now look like he'd gone home with you. He couldn't get a ride share without his phone. But he *could* call a cab from the hospital or even a nearby payphone and get a ride to Taylor's place. He could kill her and take a second cab home to you and you'd never know what he'd done. You might be a little suspicious of why it took him so long to get home but you wouldn't really question it and you certainly wouldn't volunteer to the police that he was maybe off killing your shared lover."

Meadow turned around and handed Jessie the tea in a to-go cup, though she looked like she would have preferred to throw it at her.

"There. You have your tea. Can you please leave now?"

"You bet," Jessie promised. "Just let me grab some sugar real quick."

As she poured a packet into the cup, she continued.

"Here's the funny thing though, Meadow. When I called around to see if any local cab companies had made trips from Youth Hospital to Taylor's neighborhood late on Monday night, sure enough, I found one. And then, when I asked if there were any trips from that area to Los Feliz, that same cab company mentioned a drop-off at a convenience store a mile south of your house about an hour after you left the hospital."

She took a sip of tea and waited to see if Meadow would say anything. She didn't. Instead she simply fixed Jessie with an expression that was half apprehension and half disgust. Jessie decided to go on.

"So I thought to myself—this pretty much proves that Meadow was lying about Cal's alibi. Maybe if I go in there one more time I can convince her to come clean and stop protecting him; to do the right thing for Taylor. But then, this other idea came to me. I remembered your mantra. Do you remember your mantra, Meadow?"

Meadow didn't speak. Jessie reminded her.

"I think it was something like 'We don't have any secrets. That's how we live our life.' And I thought—what if they really do live their life by that philosophy? If they do, then Cal would have told you what he did. But something about that didn't seem right to me either because that meant he'd have kept the secret about killing her from you. And *that* would violate your mantra. The only way to live by it was to discuss killing her with you beforehand."

"I think you should go," Meadow said flatly.

"No problem," Jessie agreed. "Could I get a napkin just in case this tea leaks though the cup?"

"No."

"Okay. I'll make do without. Anyway, what I was saying was that, if he was honest with you about killing Taylor before he did it, he certainly wouldn't have hidden sleeping with her from you. He's going to speak openly with you about murdering this woman but not about sex with her? I don't think so."

Meadow crossed her arms as if trying to physically protect herself from Jessie's insinuations.

"More likely," Jessie continued, undeterred, "is that he was involved in your sexual activities from the very beginning and that he lied about it because he knew she was pregnant and wanted to confuse us on the timeline. And if he knew she was pregnant, I'm guessing he probably wasn't psyched about it, what with the whole 'selfish, lack of empathy' thing. And I'm guessing you wouldn't have been super enthused either, considering your lack of fish-care skills, much less baby care. Plus, it probably didn't feel great to think that even if Cal would make a terrible father, he might have to be one to a kid that wasn't even yours. That's no fun."

Meadow sighed deeply and reached for the phone on the counter.

"I think this is the part where I call my lawyer," she said, "and tell him that there's a woman making groundless accusations against me in my own home and she won't leave."

"You absolutely should do that," Jessie advised enthusiastically. "And it's completely up to you as to whether you tell him about this other crazy tidbit I uncovered. I thought to myself—the timing doesn't really work for Cal to go to Taylor's apartment, drug her with sleeping pills, wait for them to take effect, and then catch a cab to a store near your house, all in about an hour. That a real roadblock, don't you think?"

Meadow nodded with fake enthusiasm.

"So I assume this is where you threw up your hands and decided to let the whole thing go?" she asked sarcastically.

"So close," Jessie said, snapping her fingers with her own false empathy. "No, I thought, maybe this was a longer term plan. Maybe Taylor was drugged earlier in the day and Cal just stopped by that night to make sure it had been done properly. But he's a doctor. Why would he have any doubts that he'd gotten the job done earlier? Unless he hadn't done the initial dirty deed and was just following up on someone else's handiwork. And if he wasn't the one who initially drugged her, there was only one other person with whom he shared all his secrets, right, Meadow?"

"You really are fixated on that mantra thing?" Meadow said exasperatedly, though her face suggested there was another emotion at work: fear.

"I am," Jessie agreed. "It seems really important to you guys. So anyway, I thought there was no way you'd be foolish enough to do the same thing twice. You know, have Cal drive from the gym with your phone so you'd have a personal and digital alibi while you follow Taylor from the gym to her apartment and drug and kill her. And even if you did that, there's no way the two of you would be so reckless as to use the same cab company. But sure enough, I found a logged trip from just down the block from Taylor's place that dropped a rider matching your description off at the hospital right in the time window of her death. What a wacky coincidence, huh?"

Meadow put the phone back in the cradle. She no longer looked angry. She looked stunned. Jessie pushed on, sensing her prey was close to breaking.

"So of course, I had to check with the gym. They told me you checked out around the same time as Taylor. My question is, did you sneak the sleeping medication into her protein drink at the gym and then follow her home to make sure it had kicked in? Or did you do it when you got to her place? I'm sure she invited you in and didn't have any reason to be suspicious that you'd lace her beverage."

Meadow didn't answer.

"Either way, I'm thinking you were in a rush. I checked—you had a meeting that morning that served as part of your alibi. You couldn't be late. So maybe you left before you were sure she was dead. You gave her what was supposed to be enough pills but you're no doctor and you didn't quite get the dosage right."

Meadow shifted uncomfortably against the kitchen counter. Her eyes took on the look of a deer in the headlights—wide and panicked. Still, she said nothing. Jessie decided to give her that final push.

"So you left her window open slightly and told Cal about your doubts," she suggested. "He agreed to go back and check and found that she wasn't quite dead. So he helped her along, either putting a pillow over her face or strangling her where there were already bruises from your asphyxiation games. The hope was to make it look like she'd rolled into her pillow and accidentally suffocated. Of course, most people who accidentally suffocate don't have chemical residue from surgical gloves on their face and neck, which the M.E. discovered after I had him double check a few minutes ago. But back to Cal. After ensuring Taylor was truly dead, he left, inadvertently leaving the window open in his haste. Good story, huh?"

"Just a hypothetical though, right?" Meadow reminded her.

"Maybe not so much. More of an actual thing. You see, Meadow—Cal won't be coming home tonight. He was formally charged a few minutes ago. It was pretty genius of you two to pretend to be at each other's throats as if you hated each other, but, despite that animosity, still be each other's alibis. You really sold that whole 'I hate him but I can't lie and say I wasn't with him' routine. It was so much more credible than if you were an obviously loving couple who would do anything for each other."

"You're a disgrace," Meadow said softly.

"Very possibly true," Jessie replied. "But be that as it may, my guess is that right about now, Cal's telling Detective Hernandez that this was all your idea and that he just went along to try to cover for you. He's probably admitting that those texts you sent Taylor asking why she wasn't replying were all part of your carefully constructed alibi. He's probably saying that Taylor was already dead when he got to her place so that you get charged with the actual murder and he only goes down as the accomplice."

"I doubt it," Meadow said with more confidence than Jessie thought appropriate for the situation.

"Why is that?" she asked.

"Because we don't have any secrets. That's how we live our life, remember?"

"You think that still applies?" Jessie asked, trying to determine what Meadow was playing at. Things seemed suddenly cloudier than they had only seconds earlier.

"Sure," Meadow admitted. "We were open and honest with each other about how neither of us wanted the mess of a screaming baby and visitation and child support. But then we had this brilliant idea."

"What was that?" Jessie asked, slightly confused.

Somehow things had turned. This wasn't going how it should. She felt suddenly unsure of herself and Meadow seemed to be getting cockier with each passing second. The smaller woman smiled broadly, but it wasn't the warm smile of a welcoming hostess. It was the toothy grin of a malevolent predator.

"We thought that it would be the ultimate form of connection to kill this creature together. It would be a way to solve the complication she presented and bind ourselves even tighter to one another. And it worked. It was such a turn-on. I don't think we've ever had better sex than after Cal got home that night. He was all sweaty after walking up the hill from where that cab dropped him off. It was an incredible rush."

Jessie knew this was wrong. Meadow was admitting to murder, bragging about it. There was no logical reason to do that . . . unless she thought the person she was telling could never repeat the story.

She looked down at her to-go cup and then back at Meadow, who was doing that high-energy pulsating in place thing. Then Jessie realized Meadow wasn't pulsating. She was just blurry because Jessie was having trouble focusing. She felt the cup slip from her suddenly weak fingers and bounce off the floor.

"You okay?" she heard Meadow ask from what sounded like a great distance. "You look like you need to lie down for a while."

Jessie felt her eyelids getting unfathomably heavy. Forcing them open, she turned and ran.

CHAPTER THIRTY ONE

She only made it halfway down the hallway.

At first she thought Meadow had knocked her down. Then she realized she'd tripped over her own feet. She looked up and saw the now-familiar bathroom only five feet, but still an ocean, away. She heard Meadow walking up behind her and could vaguely identify her voice.

"Good thing I had those leftover pills," she said from somewhere up above.

"Won't get...away with this," Jessie mumbled, though her tongue seemed to be getting in the way.

"That's the thing," Meadow said, seemingly regaining her bubbly disposition. "I don't need to get away with it. I just need to hold everyone off long enough to get away, period. And the authorities trying to identify the charred remains of the body in my burning vehicle while I take your car to my intended destination should give me that time. I feel awful that Cal can't come. You really messed up our plans on that one. But he'll understand. He gets me, you know?"

Jessie felt herself being lifted up by her underarms and dragged in the direction of the front door. She looked down at her leg, where her ankle holster held a small pistol. There was no way she could reach it. Instead, she tried to shake herself free but felt only a slight wriggle. Above her, she heard Meadow laugh at the feebleness of her attempt.

"Don't fight it," she advised. "If you're lucky you'll be dead by the time I light you on fire. I'm not a total bitch."

Despite the pills, Jessie felt a shiver run along her spine.

"Freeze," a new voice shouted from somewhere behind them. She couldn't see, nor could Meadow, whose back was to the voice. But Jessie was certain the voice belonged to Ryan, whom she'd called and asked to hurry over before she got out of the car and entered the Horsleys' home. "Gently place Ms. Hunt on the ground and turn around with your hands above your head."

"Oh my gosh," she heard Meadow say in a convincingly worried voice. "Thank God you're here. She passed out and I was trying to get her out to the fresh air."

"Place her down, Mrs. Horsley," Ryan repeated.

"Of course," Meadow said, reaching for something unidentifiable in her blouse pocket.

Jessie tried to warn Ryan but before she could say or do anything, Meadow dropped her unceremoniously on the floor. Her head bounced like a bowling ball and light flashed before her eyes. The only good thing about it was that the pain made her slightly more alert. Then she heard a loud thud only feet away from her.

When she reopened her eyes, she saw that Meadow was holding a Taser, which she'd apparently just used on Ryan. He lay convulsing on the ground nearby, his gun tantalizingly out of reach. A second later he stopped moving entirely.

"I'm so sorry, Detective," Meadow apologized unconvincingly. "But it looks like you're going to end up getting the crispy treatment too."

She stepped over Jessie to get to the detective, who was now her top priority. As she walked by, Jessie managed to thrust out her forearm, hitting Meadow's ankle and making the other woman lose her balance and topple over Ryan and fall splayed just beyond him.

Out of the corner of her eye, Jessie saw the woman pop up quickly. But instead of focusing on that, she trained her eyes on Ryan's gun, only inches from her grasp. She reached, attempting to grab it. Her fingers grazed, then clutched the weapon.

But lying on her back and only semi-conscious, grasping it was difficult. She could hear Meadow scurrying toward her as she flicked off the safety, glanced back behind her, and aimed the gun in the woman's general direction. She held it as steady as she could and fired once.

Meadow tumbled to the ground next to Ryan. She was clutching her upper left thigh and screeching unintelligibly. Jessie used the adrenaline coursing through her body to roll over onto her stomach, where she propped her arms in front of her and aimed Ryan's gun at Meadow, waiting for her to make an aggressive move.

After a couple of seconds, her eyes got drifty again and she considered shooting Meadow once more, this time to kill. Ryan was still in danger. If Jessie passed out, Meadow, even in her injured state, might be able to harm him.

Just as she debating whether to pull the trigger, she saw Ryan stir. He lifted his head, saw Jessie with his gun pointed at the bleeding, cursing woman beside him, and stumbled to his feet. He hurried over, grabbed his gun, and looked at Jessie with concern.

"Are you okay?' he asked. "What happened?"

With great effort, she opened her mouth, trying to ignore the sensation that it was stuffed with cotton balls.

"Drugged ... me," she said.

Satisfied that was all she could muster, she collapsed into darkness.

CHAPTER THIRTY TWO

Jessie hated Jell-O.

It wasn't so much the fault of the food. It was just that in the last couple of years, she'd spent so much time recovering in hospitals, reduced to consuming the gelatinous substance, that she could barely stomach it.

Of course, that was literally the problem this time. As the doctor had explained before leaving her current hospital room moments ago, her stomach had been pumped. That explained why her insides felt like they'd been scraped with a dull razor. It also meant her diet for the next forty-eight hours would consist exclusively of food that could be slurped and swallowed in one go.

Jessie looked around the room after the doctor left, blinking repeatedly in the hopes that her general fuzziness would disappear. However dulled her senses were, they were still sharp enough to pick up on the puke-green wallpaper and 1970s-era floral prints on her privacy curtain.

"Hey," Ryan pointed out cheerily from a chair across from her hospital bed. "At least they're releasing you today. I thought they might keep you another night."

"Another?" Jessie asked, still a bit hazy.

"Remember?" Kat said from the chair next to Ryan. "You were brought in yesterday. You stayed here last night so they could keep you under observation while they flushed all the meds out of your system."

"I have no recollection of that," Jessie admitted.

"Well, I do," Kat said, "mostly because I sat in this uncomfortable chair much of the night."

"Sorry," Jessie muttered. "Was I conscious for any of that?"

"Intermittently," Ryan said. "But I'm not surprised you don't remember much. You were pretty out of it."

"You don't look too bad, considering you got tased," Jessie noted.

"That's fairly tame for me these days," he deflected. "What do you remember? Maybe we can fill in some of the blanks."

"I remember Meadow telling me she was going to burn me up in her car. Then you showed up. She tased you. I shot her. You woke up. I conked out. That's pretty much it."

"Yeah," he said. "You definitely missed some of the good stuff."

"Like what?"

"Like Meadow Horsley handcuffed and screaming like a banshee as she was carted off to the hospital in an ambulance."

"I'm kind of glad I missed that, actually," Jessie said.

"I don't blame you," he replied. "She did *not* have nice things to say about you."

"Was one of them calling me an idiot for drinking tea she prepared after I had just strongly hinted she had poisoned someone else to death?"

"That didn't come up," he said. "But now that you mention it..."

"Leave it be, Hernandez," Jessie growled. "It's one thing for me to flagellate myself. It won't go so well for you."

Ryan looked like he might make a crack anyway but wisely thought better of it.

"Moving on," he continued, "you also missed the call we got on her cell phone an hour later from the captain of the boat she'd hired to take her and Cal from Marina del Rey to Catalina Island, where they'd chartered a private plane to fly them to Mexico."

"Now that's pretty interesting," Jessie conceded.

"I thought so too. We also got statements from all the taxi drivers giving descriptions of their passengers, which match the Horsleys. We've reconfirmed the preliminary determination that that the chemical signature on Taylor's neck matches the residue from the surgical gloves Cal used. Not that we'll need all that after the jury hears the recording you made on your phone of your conversation with Meadow before she drugged you."

"For such a detailed plan, they seem to have gotten pretty sloppy," Kat noted, shaking her head.

"Only in retrospect," Jessie pointed out. "As long as the working theory of the case was that she either committed suicide or died accidentally, everything fit pretty nicely. There was nothing immediately obvious tying them to her death. It was only once there was some scrutiny and we began to pull a few threads that their mistakes emerged. Considering that we were a few hours from bailing on the case entirely, I think their plan was actually pretty solid."

"Yeah," Ryan agreed, "and they almost got a big assist from the Propov crime family."

"What?" Kat asked, perplexed.

"We had another couple we considered suspects," he explained. "Doug and Claire Shine. Claire was gunned down yesterday afternoon and it looked like Doug might have done it to shut her up before making a run for it."

Jessie realized that she'd forgotten all about the Shines.

"Yeah, what happened there?" she asked.

"The Propovs happened. Doug Shine was found buried in a shallow grave in Will Rogers State Park this morning. We got lucky. A hiker was out on an isolated trail with her dog. He started digging up the grave. If not for that, we'd still be checking border crossings for Doug."

"So he didn't kill Claire?" Jessie asked.

"We're still putting the pieces together but Reggie Toney has a working theory. He thinks the Propovs were keeping a close eye on Doug and Claire. They might have already been worried he'd turn on them. Someone must have seen us question the Shines at the house and assumed it was about their business dealings. So they killed Claire and kidnapped Doug to see what he'd said. There was evidence that he'd been tortured. Ultimately they put two bullets in his skull."

Jessie was quiet for a moment, processing it all.

"So the Shines are dead because we questioned them?" she concluded.

"No, the Shines are dead because they got into bed with the Russian mob. This was how it was likely to end for them ultimately, whether we showed up or not."

"You're not exactly easing my guilt," Jessie said.

"Just pile it on with the rest of it, Hunt," he said caustically. "But if you want some comparatively good news, it looks like Gavin Peck isn't going to have to do his workouts behind bars."

"How's that?" Jessie asked.

"The D.A. has agreed to a suspended sentence and probation if Peck completes an anger management course and relinquishes his gun license for five years."

Jessie couldn't help but be surprised.

"The guy did wave a gun—admittedly unloaded—around a police station. I wonder what made the District Attorney's office so amenable to a reduced sentence?" Jessie asked leadingly.

Ryan gave her an embarrassed smile.

"It's possible that a detective who felt bad about baiting him into a confrontation when he was emotionally overwrought put in a good word," he said sheepishly.

Jessie glanced over at Kat.

"Who would have thought this guy was such a secret softie?" she said.

Kat smiled but said nothing.

"Oh, there's one more thing," Ryan said, clearly hoping to change the subject. "Decker apologized."

"What?"

"He'll probably want to talk to you in person," Ryan said. "But he admitted that he was rash to try to push us to close the case down so quickly. There may even be a commendation coming your way when you return in a week."

"A week?" Jessie repeated incredulously.

"Yep. He was insistent that both of us take an additional week off before coming back. I believe the exact phrase was 'to give your weak-ass, broken down bodies and your good judgment time to bounce back.'"

Jessie couldn't help but take advantage of the moment for a little dig.

"It sure is nice when a man can admit that he's been acting in an unbecoming and immature manner," she said.

The silence in the room that followed her comment was deafening.

"I think I'm going to go get some coffee," Kay finally said, standing up and quickly leaving.

The two remaining people in the room stared at each other.

"So I guess you want to talk about the other night," Ryan said hesitantly.

"Only if you do," Jessie replied with a firmness that made clear that she absolutely did.

"I acted a little weird after our kiss, I know."

"Weird is one way to put it," she agreed. "Another is head-spinningly perplexing."

"That's fair," he said quietly, looking slightly defeated.

Jessie immediately felt bad, like she was bullying the guy when he was down.

"Look," she said, deciding to let him off the hook. "I get it. You're in the middle of a divorce from someone you've spent most of your adult life with. You probably have all kinds of conflicting emotions bubbling up. Maybe you're still in love with Shelly and the idea of moving on scares you. Maybe you're not sure how you feel. This is a complicated process."

"You think that's it?" he asked, stunned.

"I don't know. Isn't it?"

"Jessie, for the record, let me be clear. I'm not pining for Shelly. That ship has sailed. I know *exactly* how I feel. I ... I'm interested in *you*."

"You are?" she asked, feeling her cheeks turn red.

"Yes."

"Then why all the middle school behavior?"

He glanced down at his feet, struggling for the words. When he looked back up, his gaze was direct.

"Part of it is, I'm out of practice with this whole flirting, romance stuff. But mostly, I'm just scared."

"Of what?"

"Of screwing it up, Jessie," he said. "I like you. But we work together. And we're friends too. I'm worried that if we try to move past that and things don't work out, it'll mess everything up. Things will get awkward and uncomfortable. And then I'll have to see you every day, knowing that not only do I not get the kissing stuff, but I've lost the friendship too. That's what I'm scared of."

Even before he was done, Jessie could feel her mouth curling into a smile. He looked so forlorn that if she'd had the strength, she would have gotten out of bed and hugged him. Instead, she made do with words.

"You worry too much," she told him.

CHAPTER THIRTY THREE

They made her leave the hospital in a wheelchair.

She was used to it by now but still found it annoying. Still, she kept her complaints to herself, remembering that it was mid-afternoon and she was being released. Spending only one night in the hospital was pretty good for her these days.

Kat pulled up to the patient entrance as Ryan helped her out of the chair and into the passenger seat. He said nothing as he folded himself into the back seat of Kat's car.

"Let's get you home," Kat said as she pulled out into traffic.

Jessie nodded as she went through the envelope that held all her stuff. She'd been changed into a hospital gown while unconscious and someone had collected her things and saved them for her. Everything seemed to be in order. Nothing was missing from her purse or wallet. She wore no jewelry so that wasn't an issue. Her phone was still charged though the battery was low. She saw that she had two messages and decided to risk listening to them, even if the phone died.

The first was from Decker, saying what she already knew. She was on paid leave for the next week. He made no mention of an apology or potential commendation. But maybe, as Ryan suggested, he preferred to handle those in person.

The second message was from a number she didn't recognize. It had a 213 area code, which covered a small area of downtown L.A. The female voice was automated and for a second, Jessie thought it was telemarketing robocall. But only for a second.

"Hello. This message is for Miss Jessie. I hope that your recovery has been without incident. I hope that you will soon be able to frolic and play with those closest to you. Friends and family are important. Relationships are fragile and like clay, are easily malleable and sometimes broken. Like you, I will soon be seeing what kind of relationship art I can create from the clay at my disposal. In fact, my work has already begun. Take care, Miss Jessie."

Even though it wasn't his voice, Jessie could still sense Bolton Crutchfield's personality in the words. The way he called her Miss Jessie, the overly loquacious verbal mannerisms, the cryptic comments that were almost always riddles.

She looked up and saw that Kat was staring at her.

"What's wrong?" her friend asked. "Your whole body just went stiff."

"I just got a voicemail with a lot of the same language as the postcard Bolton Crutchfield sent me."

She played it for them both. As they listened, she tried to discern what Crutchfield was really saying. He clearly wanted her to comprehend his true message. Maybe he was disappointed that she hadn't figured it out based on the postcard alone.

Of course, she hadn't made it a priority because he'd written in the card that she and her comrades weren't a priority for him. Since they were safe, she felt she could afford to let the message slide. But someone clearly wasn't safe. She mentally kicked herself for being so lax.

There were references to frolicking with friends and family. Twice, he'd mentioned clay and using it to create something. He was already doing it, he told her. He had said in the card that it was a pity her father had never tried it.

Jessie squeezed her eyes tight and tried to concentrate. She could sense the solution. It was right there for her if she could just find the right key. From past experience, she knew he wanted her to solve this so everything she needed to do so was already in her brain.

"I don't get it," Kat said. "And what postcard are you talking about?"

"Crutchfield had a postcard dropped off at the station yesterday," Ryan explained. "It said some of the same stuff. There was lots of talk of clay and molding. But it also said he wasn't after Jessie's friends or family."

Something clicked in Jessie's head, like a lock sliding open.

"No, he didn't say that actually," she recalled. "In the postcard, he said me and my comrades were no longer the subject of his interest. In this voicemail, he said he hoped I could frolic with those close to me. He specifically didn't say family."

"Because he knows that wouldn't make any sense," Ryan said. "He knows that your adoptive parents are dead, as well your dad, not that you'd ever frolic with him anyway."

Jessie looked at Kat, whose mouth had dropped open.

"Drive there, now," Jessie ordered.

Kat nodded, hitting the accelerator immediately.

"What's going on?' Ryan asked, confused.

"I haven't told you this but I recently found out I have another family member."

"What?" Ryan asked, shocked, before his expression morphed quickly into understanding. "That girl you were talking to?"

Jessie nodded.

"She's my half-sister. Xander Thurman was her father."

"Why didn't you tell me?" Ryan asked.

"I barely told anyone. Maybe four or five people total in the world know."

"One more than you thought, apparently," Kat pointed out. "But I don't see how he could have found out."

"That's his thing," Jessie said. "Knowing things he shouldn't. Maybe Xander told him. Maybe he did research after hearing about Xander's death. However he found out, he knows."

In her head, Jessie saw all the pieces of the puzzle slide into place.

"It makes perfect sense," she continued. "She's family but we're not close. She's young, malleable. He said he wanted to embrace the challenge of molding new clay. He said we should both pursue fresh meat—fresh faces. He was disappointed that my father didn't think to do it."

"Do what?" Ryan demanded.

Jessie looked at him, realizing that he had no idea just how deep Bolton Crutchfield's sickness went.

"He wants to train her, Ryan," she said. "He wants to turn her into a killer, like her father. He thinks she's got the right genes for it."

❧ ❧ ❧

The door of the house was wide open.

Ryan had called it in the second he understood what was going on. And as the three of them leapt out of the car and sprinted for the porch, they could already hear sirens approaching in the distance. Once there, they all drew their weapons. Jessie glanced over at the hammock, hoping to find Hannah napping there. But it was empty.

"Let me go first," Ryan said. "Jessie, you're behind me. Kat, you take rear."

"Understood," Kat said in a clipped, professional tone that Jessie wasn't used to hearing. It was like she had taken off her ill-fitting civilian costume and replaced it with her old, more familiar Army Ranger persona.

They entered the home and Jessie immediately knew something was terribly wrong. The volume on the television in some distant room was way too loud. As they carefully moved down the main hall, Jessie saw a liquid on the hardwood floor, reflected in the lights above.

At first she thought it was blood before noting it was too thin and quick-moving. It was water. She pointed it out to Ryan, who nodded silently. It seemed to be coming from the kitchen. As they got closer to the door the water was coming from, Kat indicated that she was going to loop around through what was likely the living room. Ryan nodded.

He indicated for Jessie to push open the door as he took aim. She silently counted down from three, then shoved the door open. Ryan stepped in with his weapon raised, looking for any movement.

There was none. But the source of the water quickly became apparent. The faucet was running and the sink was overflowing so that water spilled out like a small waterfall, creating a blanket of inch-deep wetness on the entire kitchen floor. Ryan moved over to the sink, his eyes darting in every direction. Once there, he glanced down, grimacing slightly before turning off the faucet with the sleeve of his elbow.

"What is it?" Jessie hissed, wanting to know what he saw in the sink.

He shook his head without responding. Suddenly the TV volume cut out, leaving only the sound of splashing water and the ever-louder police sirens.

"What's in the sink?" Jessie whispered to him again.

He paused a beat, debating whether to answer, before finally responding.

"A hand," he said. "There's a human hand shoved halfway down the sink."

A blur of movement to the left startled Jessie and she quickly raised her gun before realizing it was Kat.

"You have to come in here," she told them both. "You need to see this."

Jessie and Ryan followed her through the door into the living room. Sitting in an easy chair was a man Jessie didn't recognize. He had short black hair, glasses and wore blue jeans and a button-down shirt. His eyes were frozen open and he had a large carving knife protruding from the center of his chest.

On the love seat next to him, half-slouched on her back was a woman Jessie did recognize. It was Hannah's foster mother. She had a thinner, serrated knife jutting out of the right side of her neck. Blood, now mostly dried, had pooled on the cushion next to her. Her right hand was also missing.

"Hannah," she called out, though she knew in her bones that it was a useless endeavor, that her half-sister was long gone. "Hannah! It's Jessie Hunt. Answer me!"

In the front of the house, voices could be heard, but not Hannah's. It was the uniformed officers arriving and calling out their locations as they moved from room to room.

"Holster your weapons and get out your I.D.," Ryan advised calmly as the voices got closer. "We don't need any mistaken identity accidents."

Jessie did as he suggested, even as her thoughts turned inward.

This was Crutchfield's handiwork. And it was brutal. Somehow, despite everything she knew about his monstrous crimes and her best efforts not to be taken in by his courtly charm, she'd been compromised. She'd been lulled into complacency by his help in her life-and-death struggle with her father and his assurances that he meant her no harm.

But Bolton Crutchfield was not some friendly neighborhood scoundrel, who occasionally misbehaved but ultimately had a good heart. He was a vicious serial killer who had murdered dozens of victims. And now he'd decided he wanted a protégé. So he'd abducted one.

Jessie shook her head, trying to clear it. In moments, the house would be swarming with law enforcement and she'd lose her best opportunity to study the scene in its purest form. She took a deep breath, forced the self-doubt and guilt from her mind and got to work looking for clues that might help her find Hannah.

She looked around, her eyes clear and alert, doing her best to take in her surroundings and not be overwhelmed by the horror of them. She was so focused on studying the state of the dead bodies that it took her a while to notice the words scrawled in blood on the far wall. There were only two of them:

Fresh meat.

NOW AVAILABLE FOR PRE-ORDER!

THE PERFECT LOOK
(A Jessie Hunt Psychological Suspense Thriller—Book Six)

"A masterpiece of thriller and mystery. Blake Pierce did a magnificent job developing characters with a psychological side so well described that we feel inside their minds, follow their fears and cheer for their success. Full of twists, this book will keep you awake until the turn of the last page."

—Books and Movie Reviews, Roberto Mattos (re *Once Gone*)

THE PERFECT LOOK is book #6 in a new psychological suspense series by bestselling author Blake Pierce, whose #1 bestseller Once Gone (a free download) has over 1,000 five-star reviews.

When a man winds up dead in a hotel room in LA after a night with a prostitute, no one thinks much of it – until what seems like an isolated case turns into a pattern. It soon becomes clear that a prostitute has turned serial killer—and that criminal profiler and FBI agent Jessie Hunt, 29, may be the only one who can stop her.

A fast-paced psychological suspense thriller with unforgettable characters and heart-pounding suspense, THE PERFECT LOOK is book #6 in a riveting new series that will leave you turning pages late into the night.

Book #7 in the Jessie Hunt series will be available soon.

THE PERFECT LOOK
(A Jessie Hunt Psychological Suspense Thriller—Book Six)

Did you know that I've written multiple novels in the mystery genre? If you haven't read all my series, click the image below to download a series starter!